# Conquering

Best Wishes
Gail Huntley

# Conquering the Wild

## 1833-1912

## Book I

By

## Gail Huntley

## Cover Photo: First Sagamore Hotel, 1885
## By, Seneca Ray Stoddard

www.bookstandpublishing.com

Published by
Bookstand Publishing
Morgan Hill, CA 95037
3902_11

ISBN 978-1-61863-524-2

Printed in the United States of America

Cover illustration: First Sagamore Hotel, 1885
Photo by Seneca Ray Stoddard

Also by Gail Huntley

Blunt Force Winds

I did not plan to write this book. My plan was to capture Long Lake history from 1925-1975. After searching for books on Long Lake, I found a couple of small early history books and a few Adirondack books with a paragraph or two about Long Lake. Those books focused on boats, jobs, houses, roads, and churches. I concluded from my research that I must write a prelude to the 1925 book depicting the pioneers' arrival and the hardships they endured. Therefore, *Conquering the Wild* embraces this concept and serves as background for book II.

This is a historical novel. The author used triangulated research in order to adhere to historical facts wherever records were available. All named characters are known individuals. All dates and places are facts. The author created some dialogue and scenes in order to tell the story of the Long Lake pioneers. Descendants of historical characters are invited to correct the author should they find discrepancies.

# Table of Contents

# Introduction

There is a place cradled by the Canadian Shield, cut clean by glacier, sentineled by white birch and balsam trees, and imbued with icy blue waters. The Native Americans called it Incapaco. Incapaco was a treacherous territory, not even suitable for Native American habitat. Peter Sabattis, of the nearby Abenaki tribe, sometimes hunted in this lone Adirondack territory, but because of the cold temperatures and uninviting environment, most Native Americans lived nearer Lake Champlain. No one chose to live among the panthers, wolves, moose, and black bear until a rugged, dark haired man crawled over the dense forest in 1833 and emerged on the south end of the lake below the site of magnificent falls. His name was Joel Plumley, and he declared this land his home.

# Chapter 1

## The Plumleys

In 1832, James McCarthy, E. St John, and Colonel Sage from Newcomb reached the fourteen-mile stretch of water in the center of the Adirondacks in upstate New York. Will Hammond, who owned the lands surrounding the lake, commissioned these three men to cut a trail into the region. He had grand prospects of developing a settlement there. The three men cut a trail commencing in Newcomb at the head of Rich Lake. They proceeded for one half mile above the junction of Catlin Lake stream on the south side, following the lay of the land, snaking swamps, crossing over Fishing Brook, and finishing on a bay across from a perfectly round island.

Captain Peter Sabattis sat in his birch bark canoe waiting to transport these men to the south end of the lake. On that trip, St. John named the island diagonally across from the bay Round Island and the island further down Pine Island. This lake was a straight, narrow sheet of water, lying northeast and southwest, and in most parts not more than one third of a mile wide. The men commented on the brilliance of the red, orange, and yellow leaves juxtaposed against the deep green pines. It was a striking scene, but clearing land here would be tough work. The trees were virgin mammoths trailing so high that it was difficult to see where the treetops left off and the clouds began.

Much further south, Captain Sabattis pointed to another island on the west side, "I name her Moose Island."

St John asked, "Is that because it looks like a moose?"

"No, it's because I killed a moose there," Captain Peter replied. Later on, around the campfire, Peter shared stories of his bear and panther encounters in the depths of this untamed wilderness. That night they dined on speckled trout caught by the colonel and slept under a bark shelter built by Captain Sabattis. After dinner, they discussed the particulars of their deal with Hammond. They were to hire enough men to cut a wagon road from Newcomb to Long Lake, and St. John would construct a sawmill on a chosen site. In return for the mill and road, St John would receive five lots of land and five thousand dollars. The others would receive less. The road was to be completed before winter of 1833 and the mill completed by summer of 1834.

At dawn's light, the party paddled down the river visiting a cold spring on the east side of the lake. They stopped and inspected a stone oven, made by surveyors several years beforehand. Sabattis accompanied the party to Catlin Lake where St John paid him two dollars, making Peter Sabattis the first paid guide in the region.

In August of 1832, when St John reached Chester Village, he hired a small group of choppers (lumberjacks or tree cutters) to accompany him to the vicinity to construct a road. In addition, St John related that Will Hammond was offering fifty acres of free land to the first six families to settle in the new territory.

A dark haired man stood among the gathering. When he heard the news about free land, his first and only thought was that if he went, his family would be the first settlers in a brand new territory. His hand shot up, and he shouted, "I'm your man! I'll go. I can have my family there by spring of next year." Hence, in October 1832, Joel Plumley, E. St John, and James McCarthy travelled to Newcomb and began cutting a rough trail into the new territory. On the shore of the bay, they unloaded and began paddling down the lake in St John's bark canoe.

"Hey, St John, you told me nobody lived here. Look over there. See that smoke?" Sure enough, smoke billowed from the north end of the lake. The smoke rose high in the air cutting through the cold gray sky.

"Probably Indians," St John replied.

"Indians?" "You didn't say anything about Indians living here," Joel snapped back. For Joel, moving to this uninhabited forest meant being the first settler to do so. He liked being first and best at anything he did. While living in Vermont, Joel became the best hunter, guide, and angler in his town. However, this aggressive drive also perpetuated a life of running into and over people who stood in his way.

"Now, wait a minute, Joel. I promised that you would be the first white settler on this land, white settler." With that, Joel began paddling harder, hollering for the two men to keep up. He wanted to meet these intruders and tell them that he was here, that their hunting days on his land were over. McCarthy watched Plumley and shook his head, wondering about this intense formidable man. St John just wanted to sell Plumley some land and get away from him. Soon, they were within a couple hundred feet of a long strip of land peppered with rocks and sand. There was no one on the beach. Whoever had been there was long gone, and the smoke had dissipated.

Joel stopped paddling and looked around. There was not a canoe in sight. "Where did they go? They must have just left. We should have seen them."

"Joel, those two Indians were Peter Sabattis and his son Mitchell who hunt here. They probably went through the inlet and up Cold River," St John replied as he pointed toward the right side of the long sandy beach. By now, the canoe they were in was about 100 feet from shore.

"There may not be any Indians but look there, we got us a bear and her cub dead set ahead," McCarthy exclaimed pointing toward the left side of the beach. Sure enough, there was a mother bear swimming out ahead of her cub straight toward the three men in the canoe. St John

3

initiated a left turn toward the west shore. The bear did the same, trapping them between herself and the shore. Immediately, Joel shouldered his musket. Then a thought hit him: If I shoot her this far out, we'll be dragging her all the way to the shore. He put his gun down.

"Aren't you going to shoot?" McCarthy asked, getting his gun ready to fire.

"Naw, gonna wait until she gets closer," Joel replied. By now, the bear was fifteen feet from the canoe. One swipe of her paw and they would be in the water.

"Well, I'd rather drag her in than be close enough to smell her," St John pointed out as he pulled back the hammer on his gun and shot, hitting the bear in the shoulder. She growled in pain and moved even faster toward the boat. Now the cub began swimming out toward the mother. McCarthy did a hard back paddle, spinning the canoe southward to avoid the wounded animal. However, she also turned and in seconds was within five feet of the men. Joel stood up, stared straight into the giant black bear's eyes, and shot her. It stopped her cold, but her body floated into the canoe rocking it so hard they almost overturned. Joel reloaded and shot the cub. They dragged the two carcasses to shore, gutted them, put the meat in the canoe, delighted with their catch, and continued their trek southward. The kill would supply their families with meat for part of the winter. In this country, it was important to store plenty of dried meat because game was sparse once winter marched in. Joel looked down the long lake channel wondering how those Sabattis Indians disappeared so quickly.

Later, they reached the southern end of the lake where St John presented Joel with his land. It was positioned between a large pond and the lake. This was where Joel would build his cabin and sawmill and make a living for his family.

4

After cutting trees and putting up a lean to, the three men began taking out the trees for the cabin. They cut about two acres of land for the log cabin and cleared away a place for a dam in anticipation of starting the mill the following spring. That evening they discussed the difficulty of procuring oxen to help with the land clearing.

"Well, we could bring them up in a dugout canoe."

"Yup, long as they don't move a hair," Joel retorted. They all laughed and soon fell asleep. The next morning Joel was up at dawn. He built a fire and watched as tendrils of mist slowly recoiled from the lake. He took a deep breath. Yes, this was the place. He knew it, felt it, and lavished in it. Waking the others, he stated, "Hey, we need to cut a road from here to the East Bay landing."

"Where?" St John asked, opening his eyes and scratching his head.

"The bay. It's on the east shore. It's going to be East Bay Landing."

"Uh huh, okay, East Bay it is. Let's get started," St John replied as he rolled out of his deerskin blankets. They began that morning cutting a rough path to the landing.

Joel could not stop grinning as they made their way back up the lake to the landing and on to Chester. He could not wait to tell Sarah the good news about going to an untamed daunting place in the middle of nowhere inhabited by no one. She would love it, he thought, because it would theirs. It would be the Plumleys' territory, and they would own it all.

Of course, what Joel did not know was that St John intended to build the sawmill for Mr. Hammond. St John's eight hundred acres were adjacent to Joel's land, and St John would own the mill, not Joel. Joel knew that Hammond's offer included six men, but he knew no families would be willing to move to such a treacherous place. He knew he would be the owner of the land even though Indians hunted there. Again, he recalled seeing their smoke, but this time on the west side of the lake, just south of East Bay Landing.

Upon Joel's return home to Chester, he presented his wife with the bear meat. Then, he told her the news.

"What?" Sarah sputtered, as she spun around facing Joel, "but we just moved from Vermont." They had not been in New York State long, and already Sarah missed her family and their farm.

"But Sarah, it will be ours, and I only paid $50.00 for the land plus fifty cents for each acre. We will always have fresh meat, and you would not believe the size of the fish in those waters!"

"Fifty dollars! Joel, you spent our savings?" She ran to the jar, opened the lid, and saw it was empty. Her heart sank as fear erupted through her like a fountain.

"But the children are happy here." John was six, and Rachel only three. "Please, Joel, I don't want to go."

"No," Joel chided, "you will go. It is done!" His face began to turn the familiar red color, and Sarah knew there would be no more talk. Oh well, she thought, it can't be any worse than this town. Chester was a small town with a few families, and Sarah had managed to make one friend, a woman with a large family who lived within walking distance of her house. I will make another friend in this new territory, thought Sarah as she pushed her body away from the table.

In March, Joel returned to the land with his six-year-old son John and St John. They would prepare the site for his now pregnant wife and daughter. Sarah learned in December that she was pregnant and begged Joel to reconsider moving until the next year. However, Joel had already purchased the land and now realized that his child would be the first born in this new territory. Nothing was going to jeopardize that.

6

"Ah, Joel, this is the perfect site for a sawmill," St John remarked. "See how that point juts into the lake, and it's only a couple of hundred yards below those rapids."

"Yup, but I don't have time to put up a mill right now."

"Not you, me, I'm building it."

"No, you're not. This is my land."

"Yup, it is, but I own 800 acres over there next to that South Pond exit." St John pointed toward the stream coming out of the pond.

"But you told me I was the first settler."

"And you are, but I am commissioned to put up the sawmill. It will also benefit you. In the meantime, I will help you finish your cabin." Joel contemplated what he had just heard, realized this man could be of use to him, and handed him an axe.

"Ok, I want that tree cut for the side brace then." St John took the axe and began chopping as Joel hacked away at a tree several feet away. These men knew which trees to cut and which to spare. They cut pine, spruce, and cedar for the house construction because the wood was lighter and more resistant to rot than other trees. After Joel had cleared the site, he set it on fire. He saved the wood that remained to season for firewood. John shoveled the ashes off the site and piled them for fertilizer. They harnessed the oxen to clear the stumps and rocks and snake the logs through the woods to the site. Joel began construction with the dried logs they had cut in the fall. These created walls and pole rafters. He had battled with second thoughts about bringing John with him, but John was quite useful when it came to raising the rafters. They constructed the roof from hemlock and spruce bark. With two children and another on the way, Joel chose to have two floors. The lower floor was one large room with a stone fireplace at the south end. He put the master bedroom downstairs and the children's bedrooms upstairs in the loft. John scampered about cleaning up the shavings and catching fish for dinner.

By May of 1833, the cabin was ready for Sarah and the children. Sarah, by now eight months pregnant, endured the three-day harrowing trip in a lumber wagon pulled by oxen. She wondered whom she would meet in this new land. Joel had told her that six other families were going to be there. What he had failed to tell her was that they were not there yet.

On a sunny day in June, Sarah, John, and Joel arrived at East Bay Landing tired and half-sick from the ride.

"Only a little ways further," Joel remarked; however, this portion of the journey was extremely rough, so by the time they reached the last knoll before the cabin, Sarah had to stop several times. Finally, they pulled out into the clearing, and Sarah saw the little cabin. John jumped off the wagon and began showing her everything he had done. Sarah smiled, walked into the cabin, and sank to the ground. Joel put her on the feather bed he had made and began unloading the wagon while she slept. The next day, Sarah was up early cleaning and womanizing her new home. Soon, the aroma of venison permeated the air as the little family settled into their home perched on a clearing in a land surrounded by wolves, bears, and panthers. The baby was due in July; however, within one week of her arrival, while Sarah was sweeping up the last remnants of the sawdust created by the neverending tree cutting, she doubled over in pain. She fell to the ground, clutching her stomach and yelling for help. The men were working in the woods. John was off shooting squirrels, but four-year-old Rachel came running. "Momma, Momma!" she cried as she saw Sarah on the dirt floor.

"Rachel, Momma is okay. You go get daddy or John."

Within five minutes, Rachel came back with John. "Mom, what's wrong?"

"It's the baby, son. I am going to have the baby. Help me to the bed. Is your daddy close?"

"No. He took the boat. Oh, Momma what can I do? What can I do?" he cried.

Sarah looked over at the fireplace. Though it was June, it had been cold that night, and Joel had made a fire. "John, put another log on the fire. Go to the creek for water and put it on to boil."

"Okay, Momma," John squeaked, his little face scrunched up trying so hard to be a man in a little boy's body. Sarah knew her son and daughter should not be doing this. She cursed Joel for bringing them to this horrible spot. She watched as John followed her instructions, trying desperately to muffle her cries as the pains got closer.

"Very good, John, now I need you to run down to Mr. St John's. Tell him to find your father." With that, he was out the door as fast as a hungry wolf. Rachel checked on the water kettle hanging in the fireplace and wiped her mother's head with a cold cloth. By now, the pains were two minutes apart. Sarah knew Joel was not going to make it. She remembered the preacher and some women telling her how Indian women squatted and delivered their own babies. She rose up on the blankets, squatted, and pushed. Nothing. Oh God, please don't let this child be turned. Turned babies did not survive nor did their mothers. God, I need to be here for my children. Please help me.With that, she yelled, pushed down hard, and felt the head emerge. She cradled the head and pushed again. The baby was out! Sarah lay back exhausted hearing the first screams of little Jeremiah, the first white child born in this new land.

At that moment, Joel and John came rushing through the door. "Sarah, oh my God! Sarah, oh no; are you okay? Please, please talk to me," he pleaded as he rushed over, lifted her head, and looked in her face. Her eyes were shut. Oh my God, she's gone, he thought. Tears welled up in his eyes.

"Daddy; the baby," Rachel cried pulling at his shirt. John looked down at the tiny figure still attached to his mother. He took out his knife and cut the cord. Rachel immediately, instinctively picked up the infant and wrapped him in a quilt her mother had sewn for him. Joel ran to the well, immersed a new cloth in cold water, and began wiping the sweat off Sarah's face. His face was stark white. He prayed. "Please, God, don't take her." There was no doctor. There was no help. He looked down at her thinking my God Sarah, you were right; why did I make you come here? I could have waited a year. Why did I have to be so pig headed?

"Pig headed?" Without realizing it, Joel had muttered those words aloud, and Sarah repeated them.

"Oh, my Lord; Sarah, look at me," he whispered.

She opened her eyes, and they were the most beautiful eyes any man had a right to see. She took his hand.

"It's a boy, Sarah. It's our Jeremiah, and he is a healthy little woodsman. They had chosen that name should they have a son. Rachel has him. Rachel, your Momma is awake. Bring him." Reluctantly, Rachel brought Jeremiah to his mother. She nuzzled him tightly to her while she looked lovingly at John and Rachel. She thought how strong and mindful these two children had become. Sarah vowed never to complain again. This woodland was unforgivingly silent and deadly, but her children would mature and one day become the tenders of this magnificent space. She joined her hand with Joel's as matron of this settlement that she would call home. It was not her choice, but she would follow her husband's lead. However, in this land, joy could turn to terror in a moment prompting

10

Sarah's acceptance of her situation to wax and wane throughout the coming days.

One night while Joel was out fishing for bullhead, Sarah walked down to the creek for water. Suddenly, she heard a low growl behind her. She whipped around with the full water bucket still in her hand and stood face to face with a snarling wolf. She froze. He was between her and the cabin. He inched toward her, red-eyed, foaming, and growling. She threw the water and the bucket at the wolf, ran like a cougar for the cabin, pulled open the log door, and slipped inside slamming the door so hard it hit the wolf's nose before she heard the sound she was waiting for— the thump of the wood latch falling in place. For some time, Sarah sat with her back against the rough log door breathing heavily as her body vibrated like a whistle weed. She listened to the howling wounded creature as it dragged itself into the woods. Once again, she cursed Joel for making her come to a jungle where animals lurked behind every tree, and she had no women to talk to. It was September, the air had begun to cool, and she wondered how they would survive the winter in this treacherous place. By the time Joel returned, the wolf had wandered off, probably to die a rabid death somewhere in the deep woods. By January, the snows were so deep and winds so powerful that it was dangerous to hunt much of the time. They were starving because the scrawny corn and vegetables that had managed to poke through the black dead soil had frozen or been eaten by animals before the family had a chance to harvest much of them. Joel had worked hard that spring and fall planting oats, wheat, rye, and Indian buckwheat, but there was little to carry out to the mill in Newcomb.

Even though St John did settle and start his sawmill, business was poor. People were not flocking to the region as some of the land speculators had predicted. In addition,

11

he and Joel did not get along well because Joel was still mad at St John for being in his territory. To Joel, this was his lake, his property, and he wanted it to stay that way. Sarah longed for company and prayed for food. Somehow, they made it through that first winter, but Sarah rarely ventured outside the cabin. Food was so scarce that she once resorted to boiling bark for soup in order to warm their empty stomachs.

One day in early spring, Sarah heard Joel stomping up the porch stairs ranting about people coming here.

"People are here?" Sarah questioned, astonished that anyone else would be crazy enough to come to this place.

"Yes, there is a man building a cabin almost across from East Bay on the west side of the lake. Damn people, why can't they stay home?"

"Right," Sarah replied but smiled with glee at the thought of another family coming to the lake. "Did you talk to him? Does he have a family?"

"Yup and yup, has a mess of kids and a wife in Newcomb. They'll be coming as soon as he gets the place ready for them."

"Well, did you get their name? Who is it, and where are they from?"

They go by the name Keller. They're from Vermont like us. He and his daddy are some of them highfalutin farmers and cabinetmakers. He and another fellow by the name of Rice already started clearing. Well, we'll see. He won't make it through the winter; I can tell you that. It takes a tough man to get through the winter. He ain't tough, and he's got all them kids so the wife won't make a go of it either. They'll be out of here or starving to death the first winter."

Probably, thought Sarah, but I hope they stay. She shuddered at the thought of another winter listening to the howling wolves and wind, but something in her lifted at the thought of another woman just being near. Secretly, Joel was already envying this man for his green pastures of endless wheat and rye fields. He wondered why his wheat was growing so well. One day, he snuck onto their land, picked up a handful of dirt, and knew immediately why. It was nothing like the soil on his land. It was farmland. Joel made the decision to move. He purchased the tract next to the Kellers, began planting and building another cabin, and by July they were in their new home watching their wheat and oats come popping through the soil. This winter would be tough. Their diet would be mostly meat, but the next season would be bountiful. By the time Mr. Keller came back with his family, the Plumleys had moved in and were living next door.

**Jeremiah Plumley**

# Chapter 2

## The Kellers

"Christine, you must go on with the girls. David Jr. and I will stay to fix the broken wheel. We will catch up," David Sr. told his wife.

"But it is another eight miles through the woods," cried Christine."

"I know. You have to go with the girls because Abram will be there with the canoe waiting for us. If we don't get there before dark, he will leave." David Keller's father, Charles, and David's brother, Harmon, had visited Long Lake two years before. A young farmhand, Abram Rice had travelled with them. They came from Montgomery County where they were renting patent land. Will Hammond offered Charles fifty acres of free land with additional acreage at fifty cents an acre. Charles was elated. In November of 1832, he sent his sons, David and Harmon, on an expedition with Hammond to inspect the property. They spent two days and two nights testing the soil, later making the decision to purchase the land. In spring 1833, David, Harmon, and Abram Rice returned to plant crops. David recalled watching three men skim past him early one morning as he prepared the campfire for breakfast. That summer, they revisited making preparations for their home. The following spring, David brought his wife, eight daughters, and one son from Root, New York to Newcomb, New York. Two years later, after the men moved in and tended the crops, the family began their journey from Newcomb.

Christine Keller was excited to be a pioneer. However, in contrast to Sarah Plumley, she expected wheat flour in barrels, dried meat in the shed, and an ample amount of wood to get them through the winter. Her husband was born a farmer, and whatever he touched turned green; on the other hand, walking through these dark woods with her daughters was not something she had anticipated. If only they hadn't bogged down in that creek, they wouldn't be in this mess.

"David, are you sure we will be okay?" Christine questioned.

"Yes, but you take this gun," he advised, pulling the musket out from under the seat of the wagon. Then, to reassure her, he added, "Christine, you know you shoot better than I do. You will be fine. You have to catch Abram. David and I will have this fixed shortly, and then we will be along."

"But, daddy, Catherine cried, I'm scared."

"No need to be afraid," Christine scolded as she put her arm around her daughter. "Come on girls, let's take a walk and see if we can name the birds perched on these beautiful trees."

With that, the troupe began their descent down the trail looking up and shouting, "Momma, look, there's a blue one!"

Approximately two miles down the trail, Christine heard rustling in the bushes. She stopped. It stopped. She tightened her grip on the rifle and pressed the children to step up the pace. "Come along girls, we must get there before dark." As the afternoon waned, Sarah continued to hear movement in the underbrush.

It came as soon as they crested a large hill, a low guttural growl emanating from the left side of the woods a few feet from eight year old, Maryann. The girls all screamed at once, "Momma, what is it?" Sarah knew immediately what it was. David had told her about the panthers in this area. In Root, they did not have problems with these animals though they had shot numerous wolves and coyotes that were attacking their sheep. Sarah knew the

15

growl of the wolf. This was higher pitched than a wolf or coyote. It frightened her that this animal was lurking somewhere in the underbrush tracking them. So far, it had not revealed itself, but they all knew it was there. Christine reasoned that she could shoot the animal, but would she see it in time? "Girls, let's sing; that will keep us busy for the rest of the trip." She also figured that the noise might scare it off, though the girls' screams had not deterred it. They began to sing and did so all the way until they saw the gleam of blue water.

"Momma, we made it! We made it!" they all shouted in unison. Because dark began closing in, Sarah worried that Abram had left thinking they would come tomorrow. Her worries were valid because when they arrived at the landing, there was no Abram. To the left was an almost perfectly circular piece of land. They could barely make it out in the shadows. Sarah looked up and down the lake and began calling, "Abram, Abram!" The only sound was the water lapping onto the pebbled shore. Soon it was completely dark, and every sound sent the daughters crowding onto their mother's lap. Two-year old, Getty began to cry, and three-year-old Harriet clung to her mother.

"Shush, shush; your father will be here soon, and he will know what to do," Christine cooed as she bounced Getty on her knee. Maybe Abram went back to milk the cows and would return soon, but no one came, and the dark stayed, and soon Sarah heard the familiar rustle of the leaves and the low growl. The girls whimpered. Christine got up, pulled the hammer back on the rifle, and aimed it at the now visible slanted eyes inching steadily toward them. The gun was heavy, but fear gave her the strength she needed to stand, hold the rifle tight to her shoulder, and aim. The eyes were now only ten feet from her. The girls huddled behind a musty rotted log. The gun shook;

16

Christine shook, and just as her finger crooked to pull the trigger, the animal turned. A loud blast echoed through the forest as the animal fled, disappearing into the shadowy forest.

"Momma! It's Papa! Momma!" shouted the girls. Christine was so absorbed in protecting her children she had not heard the wagon coming into the clearing.

"Christine, I heard the shot. What was it?" David Sr. asked as he jumped off the wagon hugging the girls while staring at Christine.

"David, I shot at a panther!" she gasped as she ran to him and hugged him never wanting to let him go. Only now could she be scared, only now could she unmask her fear to him, her husband. The children could not see.

"You did great," David whispered still holding her. By now, the children were clamoring around them giggling and talking about how their mom almost shot the creepy thing, and how big and black it was, and how they never wanted to see one again. David Sr. hugged them and then asked, "So, Abram left?"

"I guess so, because we have been here about thirty minutes, and he wasn't here when we arrived."

"Darn, he probably waited, then left figuring we wouldn't be here until tomorrow." "Son, you stay here with your mother. I'll run down the trail and holler across the lake." David was already exhausted as he began making the three mile hike south through the thick forest. Finally, he reached the point directly east of his homestead and yelled for Abram. His voice echoed in the pristine mountain air, and soon Abram shouted back. In a few minutes, David heard the whooshing of paddles streaking through the calm water as Abram slowly came into view.

"Hey, Abram, where were you?"

"I waited past time for milking and figured I better get back and get the cows milked. Figured you folks weren't coming until tomorrow. I was just coming out of the barn when I heard you."

"We had wagon trouble. Christine and the girls are down at the opening. They're scared and tired so best hurry back up." With that, David stepped in the boat, and Abram whisked them away toward the bay.

"Ah, David, you know them folks that came out last year with St John?"

"Yes, the ones down the lake?"

"Well, they ain't down the lake anymore. They moved in right beside you."

"What?"

"Yup, they did; the Plumleys, and they don't seem too friendly. I never saw the wife, and that Joel Plumley; he ain't the friendly sort neither. I spoke to him one day, and all I got was a nod. Offered to help him, and he turned it down. I saw the kids, though. They got a boy, a girl, and a new one."

"Well, I'm sure Christine and the children will be happy to have neighbors."

"Uh huh," Abram responded as he began to think about seeing Sarah again. He dropped David off at the cabin and swiftly sailed across the lake to take as many as he could in his canoe. David Jr. and Harmon would take the rest with their canoes. Within fifteen minutes, Abram reached the family and loaded them into the boat, leaving the wagon at the bay. It was past midnight by the time they reached their new home. The men would return the next morning with the log raft and float the wagon and animals over. That night, Christine continued seeing slanted yellow eyes peering through the darkness before she drifted off to sleep.

Abram, David, and Harmon were up at daylight. Christine had already familiarized herself with the kitchen, found the flour and eggs, and made them all pancakes. She began making a mental note of where she would move things. She looked out the back window and noted the two cows David and his brothers had brought in. They had brought them to the landing and herded them down to the point across from the farm so the cows could swim across the lake. The chickens were easier. The children were soon out the door off to gather eggs and play tree tag.

Days and weeks went by, and Christine began to wonder why the woman next door had not paid her a visit. It was customary to call on a new neighbor. One morning Christine woke up and told Sarah that they were visiting their neighbor. Sarah made a batch of muffins and put them in a pine basket in the bottom of the boat. Since there was not a path through the woods, Christine and Sarah took the canoe and paddled around the bend to the Plumleys' landing. They pulled the canoe up on the rocky shore. Soon a little black haired boy smiling from cheek to cheek pounced upon them. "Hi, are you our neighbors?"

"Yes, we are. We've come to visit your mother." Christine knelt down to get a look at the boy. He had beautiful brown eyes and looked to be about eight years old, the same age as Catherine.

"Good, but do you got kids?"

What an inquisitive little boy, Christine thought. Sarah laughed, "Yes we have kids, and I am one of them. I am Sarah." Just then, a little girl with bobbing black curls came tearing down the bank.

"I am John, and this here is my sister, Rachel." The boy put out his hand. They shook hands and began to follow the children up the path to the front porch. John flew through the front door, "Ma, Ma, we got company!" A woman with rolled up black hair and a baby on her hip stood up and came to the door.

"Hello, can I help you?"

"Yes, we are the Kellers, your neighbors. We came to say hello." She turned to Sarah who offered the basket of corn muffins. "I am Christine, and this is my oldest daughter, Sarah."

"Oh, I couldn't take those." Mrs. Plumley pushed the corn muffins away. "Food is much too scarce here. You need to save everything you have for winter."

"We have plenty. My husband is an excellent farmer, and we have crops from two seasons so please, may we sit down and share them with you?

"I guess it would be okay. Please sit down. I am Sarah Plumley. We have lived here for two years. I see you met John and Rachel. The baby here is Jeremiah" They sat down, ate muffins, and chatted. Sarah told them about the grueling winters and the terrible conditions her family had suffered through the first winter. Within thirty minutes, they heard footsteps on the porch.

"It's Joel!" Sarah exclaimed as she jumped up. "Don't know why he's back so early."

"Hey, Sarah, everything okay here?" Joel questioned as he came through the door.

"Yes, Joel; these are our new neighbors, Christine and Sarah Keller."

"Wondered whose boat that was parked on my land." Thought it could be them Indians running around here shooting everything up."

Christine got up, walked over, and put her hand out. "I'm pleased to meet you, Joel. What do you mean about Indians shooting everything?"

He shook her hand and then began, "Ain't safe here. Them Indians could get you in your sleep, you know."

"No, Joel, I didn't know." Soon after, Christine and Sarah left. Both women were disturbed by how Joel described the Indians.

20

A few days later Christine met Peter Sabattis and his son, Mitchell, the ferocious Indians. That is when she began to understand something about Joel Plumley.

That was the first, but not the last, encounter with Joel Plumley. Christine learned that Sarah Plumley rarely went out and that Joel Plumley liked it that way. David also approached Joel but quickly learned that he was not the neighborly type. Consequently, the only two families settled in this mountainous country kept to themselves, except for Abram Rice and Sarah Keller who grew fonder of each other every day.

J. F. HOLLEY.                                    CHESTERTOWN, N. Y.

**Sarah Dornburgh Keller and David Keller, Jr.**

# Chapter 3

## The Sargents

In the winter of 1834 James Sargent, a carpenter in Waitsfield, Vermont, heard that the landowner, Will Hammond, was selling large lots of land in northern New York for fifty cents an acre. James had married his childhood sweetheart, Betsey. He adored her and vowed to take care of her for the rest of her life; however, Betsey's numerous friends troubled him, especially her old beau, Patrick, who still lived in the same town. This new venture seemed the perfect opportunity for him to take his Betsey away from this man.

One night, as they that sat by the fire, he approached her with the idea, "Betsey, they got this land for sale south of here in New York State, and it's real cheap."

"Oh, how cheap?" Betsey asked.

"We can get fifty acres free, and buy more for fifty cents an acre. We could own so much more land there than here."

"Why would land be free? What's wrong with it? Betsey asked.

"Nothing. It's just not settled yet."

"James, what will we do? How will we live? How will I speak with my family? What about the children?"

"He looked over at his oldest daughter, Mary, with her long blonde braids and big blue eyes. She was kneeling on the rag rug holding yarn for her mother. James Jr. sat on the floor pushing a spool toy James had made him for Christmas. "The children will love it. It will be an adventure," James responded quickly. However, he felt a twinge of fear in his throat. Immediately, he replaced the fear with visions of his family in a snug cabin in the wilderness with crops multiplying like dandelions in the fertile soil. Haven't I always provided for you, Betsey?"

"Yes, but…"

"There! You see, we will be fine." He patted her on the knee and went off to bed.

Betsey sat in the pine rocking chair James had made for her when she was pregnant with Mary. She feared leaving all she knew and wandering into the wilderness. She had heard stories about this place, racked with craggy mountains and vicious animals. She felt safe on the farm where she grew up. In the spring, they planted crops and prepared all summer for the bitter cold winters. In February, they made maple syrup and sold it to the neighbors, but in this new territory, how would they eat? How would they survive the winter?

In March of 1835, the Sargents made the horrendous journey down the worn path. At East Landing Bay, Mitchell Sabattis met them and guided them to lot 82, at the start of the lake. When the children saw the log cabin, they quickly tumbled out of the wagon and scattered through the house like a pack of dogs. Betsey was less than thrilled. She wondered if she would ever get used to living in this small space, but James was excited. Seeing the look of pride on his face, Betsey pushed her skepticism aside and resolved to accept living here. After all, what could happen? There were only two families here. She could shoot a gun, and there were endless fish in the lake, so they would not starve. Their property began at the outlet of the pond. Betsey loved the idea of owning so much land. She would make a home here for her family.

The next evening Betsey and James paddled up the lake in their canoe. James pointed to a house on the west side of the lake, "That is where the Kellers live. There are several daughters and one boy."

"Oh, James, can we call on them?"

"Betsey, I don't know that we should," but just then David Keller came out the front door onto the porch. "Hello," he called and waved them in.

"Hello," Betsey yelled back.

"Are you the Sargents?"

"Yes," James replied.

"Come on in for a spell. I am David Keller." With that, James and Betsey launched the canoe toward the west shore. Before landing, they keenly observed what appeared to be a whole village pouring out of the Kellers' front door. They all lined up on shore, and soon a black haired woman swollen with child joined them. Once James and Betsey stepped out of the boat, David Keller made the introductions and released the children who quickly scattered off to play in the woods. Christine invited them in for tea.

Betsey immediately liked Mrs. Keller. She was strong, confident, and willing to talk. After the men went off to the shed, Betsey and Christine settled into the kitchen. "Where are you from?" asked Mrs. Keller.

"Vermont."

"Oh, we are too. First we went to Root then here"

"We lived on my parents' farm," replied Betsey. Do you ever feel closed in here?" The land is cleared and pastured, but those monstrous pine trees surround us. Sometimes I feel completely fenced in.

"I know what you mean. You will get used to it. Sometimes I paddle out to the middle of the lake just to feel the openness. Now, missy, can you shoot a gun?"

"Yes, my father taught me. We used to kill gophers and crows on the farm to stop them from eating the crops. By the way, Mrs. Keller, how many families live here?"

"It's Christine, and two families live here. The Plumleys are next to us, but they aren't too friendly.

Betsey, why don't you come visit me one afternoon and we will quilt."

"But how?

"Well, by boat of course. Just put the little ones in the boat and paddle on down, dear. Don't you know how to paddle a boat?"

"Uh, I don't know, never tried. I never needed to on the farm, and I don't know if James would let me."

"Let you? Dear, you had better learn. Living here means learning all about the woods and the water. Best you learn how to live here than die here."

Soon James and David returned, and the Sargents headed home. As they passed the shoreline, Betsey pointed to the cabin and told James that the Plumleys lived there. She felt better just knowing other women on the lake, but Mrs. Keller's warning disturbed her; best you learn how to live here than die here.

The following week, James commenced cutting trees for the garden. He wanted to plant early, but it would be tricky just like in Vermont--planting too early could be fruitless if there were a mid-May frost, but setting seeds too late may not allow for a long enough growing season. That afternoon, Betsey prepared rabbit stew for dinner. The luscious smell of meat permeated the cabin, and Betsey hummed as she set the table. She was an adapter. Betsey had the mind to adjust to whatever came her way. She looked out the window at the afternoon sun sprinkling diamonds on the blue lake waters, and she thought, I am going to like this place, and she did until 5:30, when James was still not home. James was methodical, always back by 5:00 for supper. Betsey went out on the front porch and yelled for him. He did not answer. She ran in and told Mary to stay in the house until she returned. Betsey figured about where he would be and began walking yelling his name. Suddenly, a great foreboding overcame her. She looked around seeing only the black wood trees and the failing sun playing tricks on her vision. As the light passed through the thick tree trunks, she thought she saw James peering out or an animal's tail disappearing and reappearing behind the towering maple trees. She finally reached the little clearing. By now she was running, and shouting his name, "James, James, where are you?"

The silence of the woods was deafening. She began to panic thinking oh my God; maybe he went down the lake and had an accident. She ran to the shore, but the dugout canoe was exactly where James had left it the night before. Would James have ventured further into the woods? Maybe, but where? She ran back to the cabin, grabbed the shotgun, and began progressing deeper into the woods. First, she headed south shouting his name as she scanned behind each rock and mossy knoll. Soon, she could hear the rumble of the great falls. She turned and headed back to the house, this time walking north on the wagon path they had traversed many weeks before. "James, James!" she hollered frantically.

"Betsey."

Betsey stopped. Had she heard her name, or was it just the whistle of the west wind piling into the evening forest? She could not be sure. Once again, she heard the soft husky voice, "Betsey, over here."

She turned toward the sound, took three steps into the woods, tripped over a fallen log, and landed on the ground next to her husband's body. She screamed, "James, oh my God, James!" She pulled herself up, dropped the rifle, and bent over him. He was face down, and she could barely see him among the pine fronds. A mammoth white pine branch had pinned him down. Betsey grabbed the heavy branch, stood up, and tried to lift it.

26

"Betsey, you can't lift it off me. It only has my hand, but I cannot get it out. You will have to cut me out of here."

"What? No, no, I can't. What if I miss and cut you?" She had used an axe but was not proficient at cutting.

"You won't. I'll tell you how to do it. It is the only way. Now, pick up the axe."

Betsey looked it over. He was right. She only had to cut through the branch, but a branch the size of a tree. She picked up the axe and began to examine the situation. She scanned the black round cylinder looking for where she would cut to avoid any more harm to James. She looked back at her husband. He was silent. She ran to him. "James, James," she whispered as she kissed his neck. He did not move. He had passed out. She picked up the axe and swung it high above her head, coming down with all her strength, watching the blade sink its teeth into her target. An hour later, she pulled the branch off her husband's hand and managed to drag him into the house. Betsey laid him on the cot and looked at his mangled hand. She knew it was broken in several places. What could she do? There was no doctor. There was no medicine to tend the wound other than to clean it. She went outside, grabbed a branch, stripped it, put it on his wrist, and ripped off a piece of cloth. Betsey tied this around the branch and his wrist, making James a splint. She had to get help. "James, James, she whispered as she patted his face with a cold cloth.

"Betsey," James opened his eyes. "Oh, Betsey, did you…but how?"

"Honey, there is not time for that now. I am going to the Kellers for help. I don't know how to set a splint, but I am sure Christine does."

"No, I don't want you out in that boat by yourself," James retorted weakly trying to get up but falling back down.

"James, there is no other way. I have to get help." By now, James was unconscious again. "Mary, you stay here with your father. Keep him covered. Go get a jug of whiskey from the barrel. He will need it when he wakes up." Betsey looked out the window. Dusk was settling in. She knew she must leave now before darkness.

She hustled out the door, threw the gun in the canoe, and pushed off. Betsey stepped into the boat, and it immediately tipped. Quickly, she centered herself before the canoe tipped over. She reached for the paddle, and it threatened to dump her again. Oh Lord, how will I get all the way to the Kellers when I cannot even keep it steady for a few minutes? Betsey had always just sat there looking over the reflection of the majestic conifers in the pure indigo lake waters. She no longer had that luxury. Tonight, she had to remember how James did it. She thought about how he sat straight in the seat and seated the placed paddle in the water without hunching or moving. She sat up straight and pulled the paddle through the water. The canoe began to move. She held her breath for the second stroke and the third. Paddling was precarious, to say the least. When she paddled to the right, the log boat tipped so roughly that she quickly pulled the paddle out of the water. She sat stock-still, took a breath, and put the paddle in again. She stroked the water gently, barely making a dent in the vast mirror below her.

At this time of night, the lake was a gentle giant as if settling in for the shadowy night. Soon Betsey conquered the rhythm, slowly shifting the paddle from left to right, steadily floating up the lake. Shortly, she came to the Plumley place. She thought of stopping there but remembered Christine's remark about how unfriendly they were, so she whisked off until she entered Kellers' bay. Just ten feet off shore, Betsey began shouting, "Mr. Keller, Mr. Keller!" Once again, the whole clan tumbled out of the house, loud footsteps clanking on the porch boards. David Keller Jr. reached her first, pulling her boat up on shore.

"What's wrong, Betsey?" He knew by the pinched look on her face that something was wrong. By now, David Sr. and Christine had arrived.

"It's James." Betsey tried to breathe. She was exhausted from the trip.

"Hold up, little missy, catch your breath and then tell us," Mrs. Keller cautioned as she put her hand on Betsey's shoulder to calm her.

"I'm okay, but James is hurt. I need help. A tree fell on his arm. I don't know what to do."

Christine replied, "We will come. David Jr., get the boat ready. I'll get bandages and salve. Betsey, did he break his arm?"

"I am not sure if it's his arm, wrist, or hand, but I think it's broken."

"Okay, we will bring a splint for him." Christine ran into the house, grabbed the straight piece of wood she had sawed and whittled for breaks. She had several lengths of wood ready in waiting. Since there were no doctors for miles, Christine had learned to be prepared. Though neither she nor David drank alcohol, she always kept some on hand. She grabbed the dusty bottle, along with strips of cloth and homemade salve, rushed out the door, and told young David to keep an eye on the children. David Sr. jumped in his boat and within minutes was sailing past the Plumleys. Betsey and Christine worked their boat much more swiftly than when Betsey came down the lake by herself. Finally, Betsey allowed herself to feel. Tears welled up in her eyes, and she began to cry. Oh, God, she prayed, please let him be okay. By the time they arrived, James had regained consciousness. Christine looked at his wrist, touched it, and he winced in pain. "Yup, a broken wrist." She put the alcohol up to his lips and told him to drink. He started to protest, but it was short lived as Christine was a formidable figure with her large frame, fiercely pulled back hair, and straight arrow dark eyes. Christine cleaned out the wound with alcohol, splinted his wrist, and David told them he would be back with David Jr. to do the chores in the morning.

"No," James whimpered, "You have too much to do yourself. Please, Mr. Keller, I'll be okay in a few days. It will be okay."

"Young man, I don't think so, but it's up to you. Come on, Christine; let's let these two get some rest." James repeated his thank you, and Betsey escorted them down to the shore, thanking them profusely and vowing secretly to make pies the next day to take down to this wonderful family.

Mr. Keller's premonition was right about recovery. James tried to swing an axe the following day, but he could hardly stand much less hit anything. Betsey did what she could, but she knew that if they failed to plant their vegetables now, the first fall frost would kill them. They needed the harvest to survive the desolate winter. Betsey had heard of people starving to death in the wilderness because once the snow came travel could be difficult.

"James, you have to bring your brother here to help us," Betsey chided one morning as James sat feeling helpless, angry, and frustrated about the situation they were in.

"No."

"But, why not? He wanted to come in the first place. He offered to come and help us. We need him now. Please, James."

"And why do you want him here so badly?" James retorted.

"For God's sake, to help us, so we don't starve to death!"

30

"No, I'll not have my him living here!" James yelled back.

Betsey began to cry. She ran down to the water, pushed out the canoe and began paddling.

James struggled after her yelling, "Where are you going? Betsey, get back here!"

"I'm going to the Plumleys and the Kellers and ask them for help. I am not eating bark this winter because of your pigheadedness!" Betsey shouted back, her words echoing off the mountains.

"No, Betsey, please; don't drag our neighbors into this. Ok, ok, I'll fetch Robert. Now, get back in here before the neighbors hear us."

Betsey laughed, "Neighbors, you mean the trout and the trees?" She paddled back in and helped James up to the cabin.

The next day, they began the journey over the bumpy forty-mile trail to Chester to post a letter to Robert. Betsey visited the general store, longingly looking over the bright gingham and calico, dry goods, and food they could not afford. She thought, why couldn't we have settled here where there is at least some civilization? However, she knew that had they settled in Newcomb or Chester, they could not have purchased so much acreage. Soon they were heading back home where Betsey immediately began clearing the land. As the days past, she became stronger. Her pale skin burned bronze; she tossed off her bonnet; the first morning the tie wrapped around her arm as she was cutting, and she almost cut her leg off. Every night, she fell into bed exhausted, dreading the next morning when she would get up and repeat the day before. James was melancholy, though he was able to do some of the planting. As tiring as the work was, there were some mornings when Betsey, watching the spectacular purple sunrise on the mountain, would take a deep breath and consume the aroma of the balsams, spruce, and hemlock, and in that moment she would wish to be a man. She loved being outdoors and now realized that should she do these chores for long, she would prefer them to the endless cooking, knitting, sewing, soap making, and cleaning that was woman's work.

Three weeks later, Betsey and James were clearing more land. James was still using one arm, supervising, and hauling brush with the oxen while Betsey cut. They were a team, and James admired the way his wife had adapted to this rugged way of life. Betsey pulled back on the axe, ramming it into a resilient red spruce. "Hold it, Betsey, I hear something!" James shouted. Betsey stopped the axe in midair.

Yes, she heard it too--clip clop, clip clop. "It's a horse, James! It's got to be your brother!" They both ran down the trail and watched as Robert crested the hill. "Robert," Betsey yelled." Hello!"

"Hello!" Robert shouted back shielding his eyes to see against the morning sun. Soon he and his horse, Babe, were in full view. James recalled how delighted Robert was when their father came home with that young colt. This was Robert's birthday present, and he loved this horse more than he loved anything. Robert trotted up to them, hopped down, and hugged James and then Betsey. He looked at his brother's arm, still bandaged. "Looks like you got yourself a real good excuse for making me do all the work." He laughed. James did not laugh. "Come on, James; you know I'm joking. I am glad you posted me, and I am ready to start. Betsey, you look like you got yourself some sun."

"Yes, I've....

"Yup, Robert, she's been bringing in the fish and learning to paddle the boat," James cut in. Well let's get up to the house and get you something to eat. Thanks for coming, Robert."

"Sure enough," Robert replied as they walked up the path. "Wow, James, nice place you got here." According to your letter, you need me to finish clearing, burn over, ash the garden, and plant oats, wheat, and rye."

"Right," Betsey replied. "We started the planting, and among the three of us, we should be able to get it finished and planted within the next two weeks."

"No," James snapped. "Betsey, you can help later with the planting, but you will not be helping with the clearing."

"But…."

"You will not be helping!"

Robert looked from his brother to his sister-in-law, moved nervously from one foot to the other, and thought, James hasn't changed. From the time they were young boys, James had always wanted whatever Robert had. He remembered how mad James was when Dad brought home Babe, even though James had his own horse. Robert was not one to back down, so the two boys had several scuffles growing up, but Robert loved his brother, and James needed his help, so here he was. Two weeks later, they had cleared the ground and seeded. Betsey chinked the house with moss and clay to prepare for winter. She also kept the coals hot in the fireplace by covering them with ashes. It was vital for survival that the coals always stay lit because if not, they would have to go to the Plumleys or the Kellers to bring home live coals. James would have despised doing that. In addition, Betsey had prepared a bed in the loft for Robert and cooked the meals every day.

Robert soon met the Plumleys and the Kellers, especially Jane Ann Keller. He recalled the first time he saw her, running down to the shore with her brother, David, to see who he was. A new visitor created much excitement in the small community. Before Robert reached shore, Mrs. Keller and all the kids were there to greet him. He was immediately scared of Mrs. Keller as she shuffled her flock behind her, and asked, "What may we do for you, mister?"

Robert stared at the shotgun placed strategically across this woman's stomach. It was loaded and ready to fire.

"Uh, just paying a friendly visit, Mrs. Keller; I'm Robert, James Sargent's brother."

"Oh, and what's his missus name?" she asked sternly.

"Momma," Jane chided, embarrassed at her mother's harsh treatment of this man.

"No, no, that's okay; her name is Betsey, and James broke his arm, so I am here to help them."

"Good enough for me. I'm Christine, and this is Sarah, Jane Ann, David, Maryann, Catherine, and Rachel." The girls all nodded their heads. David shook his hand. "Mr. Keller is up in the field. Would you like to come in for a spell?"

"Well, I wasn't…."

"Oh, come on in. At least let me get you a drink," Jane replied. She could not take her eyes off this handsome man.

"Okay, I could use some water, but then I'll be on my way." Jane was petite and friendly. She reminded Robert of Betsey except Jane was younger. Mrs. Keller began telling him about their arrival and how he should stay to meet Mr. Keller. Soon, Robert's fear of Christine abated, and he felt happy around this welcoming family. He could not wait for David because he had one more stop to make before heading home.

As he stepped out of the door, Mrs. Keller invited him to return for supper one night and meet David. He vowed to do so, thanked her, and pushed off down the lake to visit the other neighbor, Joel Plumley. Robert steered the large wood canoe to within ten feet of their shore and

34

hollered, "Hello, hello there, I'm Robert Sargent!" All was silent on this homestead. Hmm, he thought, must have gone down the lake. As he pulled back on the paddle maneuvering left out of the corner of his eye he saw a face peering out of a window; however, just as quickly, it disappeared. Hum, must have been the sun casting a shadow, he thought as he dug in his paddle and proceeded on down the lake. Behind him, in the shadowy dusk, Joel Plumley stepped out from behind an ancient spruce, gripping a heavy percussion double-barreled rifle. He lifted the weapon to his shoulder, aimed it directly at Robert, and whispered into the silent silver water, "Bang!"

# Chapter 4

## Zenas Parker and Barton Burlingame

Zenas Parker, unmarried, thirty-two-year-old adventurer and farmer from Vermont, arrived in Long Lake in 1836 and settled on the west side of the lake opposite the new mill built by St John. He and a friend, Barton Burlingame, immediately began clearing the land.

After two days of back-killing work clearing trees, digging up roots, and sleeping in the rain under a makeshift pine bough shelter, Barton exclaimed, "I ain't staying here, Zenas. This isn't farmland. It never was and never will be. I'm going back to civilization."

"No, Barton, you can't. Come on. Don't give up. Stay a little while longer, at least until I get the main timbers cut. I can't do it alone." Barton looked at his old friend. They had grown up together. He knew that, for years, Zenas had wanted to go away on his own, but he had stayed because he felt obligated to his parents.

As soon as his brother was old enough to help with the farm, Zenas had announced that he was leaving. Now he recalled their first visit to claim their land. The massive virgin pines, maples, and beech trees towering over his property amazed him. He loved the pungent odor of these primeval woods. As they whisked down the lake, Zenas noticed that the giant sugar maples that jutted up rounded to the sky. These reminded him of Vermont; however, the vivid green evergreens sighing into the hardwoods on a breezy day were a phenomenon that astounded him. "Look, Barton, look at those colors. Never seen anything like that back home."

"Nope, never did," mimicked Barton. Zenas was determined to work this land, and Barton was determined to be wherever Zenas settled, so the following spring, they returned with two oxen, a sleigh, and supplies to last until the cabin was up. They used oxen because these animals could pull the stumps out of the ground, and they were more surefooted among the stumps and rocks of this landscape than horses were.

Barton figured that fifty logs, of ten inches in diameter would provide for the sides of the sixteen by twenty-four-foot cabin. They cut large cedar logs for the sills on which the walls rested. Then, they positioned the logs on flat stones in the dirt. It was while they were erecting the pole rafters that they noticed two men soaring down the ice-skimmed lake. Zenas waved, and they waved back. Barton shouted, "Hello."

"Hey," was the reply. Zenas waved the men in, watching them back paddle as they turned the boat toward him. Barton and Zenas walked down to the lake carrying their guns. The men in the dugout canoe stepped out and pulled the craft on shore. "Good cabin you make here," stated the older man. They were both dressed in leather pants and moccasins. They were dark skinned, dark eyed men with prominent noses and round faces.

"Good Morning," Zenas said. "I am Zenas Parker, and this is my partner Barton Burlingame. Do you folks live here?"

"No, only hunt here. I am Captain Peter Sabattis, and this is my son, Mitchell." Barton and Zenas relaxed the hold on their guns and invited the pair up to the lean to. "Why you come here?"

"We came for the land. We plan to do some farming."

"Farming, huh; don't know about that but fishing and hunting are good here." With that, Peter Sabattis poked the younger boy, and the boy went back to the canoe and pulled out several impressive brook trout.

Barton stepped forward to get a better look. They were beautiful fish, maybe the largest trout he had ever seen. "Holy cripes, where did you get trout like that?"

"We have come to bring you fish. We will go now."

"But, can't you stay and eat these fish with us?" He could not believe they would just bring fish and leave.

"No, they are for you. We will have more. We will see each other again." He turned, softly stepped into the boat, and silently paddled away.

Zenas held up the fish and looked at Barton, "We got us a big dinner tonight." He turned and watched as the floating log disappeared into the sunset. Hmm, he thought, the people here are okay. They had already met the Sargents, discerning that Betsey was an excellent cook, Robert an outgoing happy go lucky type, and James, though somewhat somber, seemed a nice enough man. He delivered a delicious loaf of bread from Betsey, explaining that his wife was shy and did not like strangers around the house. Zenas assured him that they would not disturb her, thanked him for the bread, and asked him to stay a spell. James declined and soon was off, leaving the two men delighted with their bread and feeling good about their neighbors. Two days later, Robert Sargent arrived and helped them with the roof and some of the clearing for pasture.

The next day Abram Rice and Sarah Keller came with vegetables and an invitation to come to their house on Sunday. Abram worked for Mr. Keller and from what Barton saw, he had an eye for Sarah; however, after meeting her, so did Barton. During the visit, Barton tried to speak but could not. Nothing he thought of to say made sense when it reached his mouth, so he remained mute except to say good-bye at their leaving. After they had gone, Zenas remarked about how inhospitable Barton was the entire time the guests were there. Barton's response was, "I like that girl."

"Well, you sure are doing a good job of chasing her off for liking her," remarked Zenas.

On Sunday, Zenas and Barton began the journey up the lake to the Kellers'. They turned into the bay, pulled up the boat, walked up to the cabin, and knocked on the door. Abram opened the door and greeted them. They walked into the log cabin, and Abram introduced them to David and Christine Keller, James, Robert, and Betsey Sargent and several of the children. Though he had met James and Robert, this was the first time Zenas had seen Betsey. What a pretty girl she was. Barton managed to say hello and thank Sarah for visiting them earlier.

"Oh, it was Abram's idea; there are so few neighbors here that a new one is always a welcome sight."

"Is this all of us? Is this all of the settlers so far?"

"No," Maryann piped up. "The Plumleys have the cabin you passed before ours.

"Quiet folks," was all Mrs. Keller offered. Then Zenas told the story about the two men and the fish, and David explained that Peter and his son did not live in this town but they hunted and fished in the area.

Dark was falling when Zenas and Barton returned to their boat for the paddle home. Zenas thought about David, Christine, James, and Betsey and wondered how he would ever meet a wife in this womanless jungle. The only women here were those who followed their husbands, and in the years since Christine Keller arrived, only the Sargents had stayed. Well, he thought, I guess I'll be living alone because I sure ain't leaving this place.

On the other hand, Barton was already scheming as to how he was going to make Sarah Keller fall in love with him, Abram Rice or no Abram Rice.

# Chapter 5

## Decisions in a Dangerous Land

Joel Plumley walked through his sparsely planted field. He wished he had moved to this spot when he first arrived. He thought of the families trying to make a living at the head of the lake. Oh well, better them than me. He knew they settled there because of the sawmill. He laughed to himself as he thought of that ridiculous endeavor by St John. Some sawmill! He only finished half of it before winter hit last year. Due to the heavy snow, and the blasting spring rains, the contraption kept washing out. Now, St John was threatening to move since few people who came had remained. He was a businessman and business was not booming, which was good news to Joel. He could tolerate Captain Peter and Mitchell, but the rest of them could go back to where they came from for all he cared. Four-year-old Jeremiah ran out of the house and grabbed Joel's leg.

"Papa, can I go to the barn with you today?"

"No, son, I got business to attend to. Now, you stay with your Momma. John, you can go up and milk the cows. I have to leave for a few hours."

"Okay," John turned and headed up to the barn. Joel set out for the pond, which they now called South Pond. He had heard that several other families were coming in soon. He had heard it from Keller who heard it from St John. David Keller, was an okay man and a hard worker, but that did not make Joel like him any better than anyone else. Joel had talked with him about keeping those kids off his property. Pulling the boat up on shore, Joel walked up the hill to the mill where he saw St John standing around watching his helper rebuild the mill. Typical, thought Plumley that man don't do a lick of work he doesn't have to do.

"Hey,"

"Hey," St John replied and turned to face Joel.

"What's this I hear about more people coming here?"

"Yup. I hope it's true. I brought a man in last week who might settle."

"Is that right? How soon do you think that will be?"

"Don't know. He was looking at the lot about a half mile down the road."

"Uh huh. Another farmer?"

"Don't know. Know he builds boats."

"Well, you can't eat boats, so let's hope he can't grow anything and high tail it out of here after the first winter."

"Yup, can't blame um if they do. Last winter was the worst yet."

"And Keller says this winter is going be a bad one too."

"He's usually right."

"Uh huh. Hey, I have to get back to the farm. I'm putting up a new fence next spring, so I'll be back in the fall to get some logs cut."

"Ya," St John answered; he knew there would be no cutting timbers for Plumley in the spring because he planned on getting out of this God forsaken place before another winter set in. This would leave the little settlement with no sawmill, but St John couldn't do anything about that; business was business.

On the way back to his place, Joel passed by Barton. Barton tipped his hat, "Hey, Joel." Joel did not answer. Barton wondered why a man would be so unfriendly to his only neighbors. Folks needed each other out here. Barton's thoughts about Joel were short-lived. He was on his way to see Sarah Keller, and not even Joel Plumley's cold stare could dampen his elation. At times, he was known to wallow in the darkness, especially when he drank too much whiskey. Barton and Robert Sargent had become friends and business partners. They made whiskey and beer and sold them to the neighbors. The Kellers didn't drink, but Plumley and Captain Sabattis were good customers.

He met Sarah on the porch, and she looked especially pretty with her hair down and braided. He was glad she did not wear the bonnets that some of the women still wore. He loved the way the sun skated across the red streaks in her coal black hair.

"Hi Barton, it's good to see you. I am looking forward to this outing."

"I am too, and you look very nice today." Barton responded as he took her arm and started leading her down the path.

"Well, thank you, Barton; that is kind of you to say." Sarah looked behind her at Catherine, "Now Catherine, don't spill the tea."

"Catherine?" Barton asked.

"Oh, yes;" she wanted to come too. You don't mind do you, Barton?"

"Uh, uh, no, guess not. Sure, come on Catherine." Of course, he minded. He wanted, for once, to see Sarah alone. Soon they were at the bay on the east side of the lake where the fishing was good. Catherine caught the first fish.

"Oh," she squealed with delight as she yanked the line and pulled the fish in. By two o'clock, they had caught enough for lunch. They paddled ashore, built a fire, and Sarah cooked the fish. When they had finished eating, she got up, picked up her fishing pole, and declared, "I'm going to get a few for Papa, Momma, and Abram."

This was his chance to find out more about this Abram fellow. "Uh, Abram, he is your father's hired hand, right?"

"Yes, he is," Sarah answered.

"And Sarah's husband," Catherine exclaimed.

Barton froze. Oh my God, husband. He knew Abram was David's farm worker. It had never occurred to him that Abram and Sarah might be married. Somehow, he managed to blurt out, "Yes, I heard," but he was devastated.

"Yes, Barton, and you just missed the wedding. We were married last year by the visiting preacher." Barton was speechless. A heavy sadness overtook him that he could not hide. He feigned illness and within thirty minutes was on his way back home.

Once home, Barton went to the shed and headed straight to the whiskey barrel. Zenas was working in the field that day. Barton drank his fill and then decided to cut firewood. Chopping wood always made him feel better. He headed south on Sargent land (by now they owned many acres) and began cutting on a large spruce. He swung the axe, cursed his life, cursed Abram, and swung again. Soon the mammoth tree was ready to fall. Barton pushed on it. It began to fall; however, in his anger and drunkenness, Barton had made the wrong cut and in a split second the giant tree was falling straight toward him. He spun around, running as fast as he could run, but a large branch caught him across the legs.

In the meantime, Zenas came back from the field and prepared supper thinking that Sarah must have invited Barton to dinner. Later on that evening, Zenas strolled down to the lake to catch some bullhead. He noticed Barton's boat floating in the brush, one end of it already licking the lake waters. He secured the boat and wondered why Barton would have left it there. He reasoned that Barton must have come home. If so, where was he? Zenas returned to the house and shouted Barton's name. Silence called back. He walked straight to the shed behind the cabin, opened the door, and looked to the right. There was Barton's gun leaning against the wall in its familiar place. That's strange thought Zenas. Looking straight ahead to the northeast corner of the shed, he noticed that the whiskey barrel cap was ajar. Zenas looked back at the gun. Barton would never go anywhere without his gun. As his gaze hit the whiskey barrel again, a sense of dread began to consume him. He ran to the front porch. The axe was missing! Oh no, Barton, you didn't get drunk and wander off into the woods to chop wood. Many men took a swig of whiskey to ease the chill of the morning air; however, Barton rarely took one swig of anything. Besides, he could hardly walk when he drank, much less swing an axe. Now Zenas was sure that Barton got it in his inebriated head to go off and cut.

Zenas criss-crossed the property shouting, "Barton, Barton, you out there?" He followed the trail north to where he had cut most of the trees for the cabin, constantly shouting Barton's name. His only reply was the knocking of a pileated woodpecker's beak on the red pine above his head. As daylight descended, he debated whether to continue his search or go to the Sargents for help. He went back past the house, this time heading south shouting Barton's name. Still nothing.

James Sargent, hearing Zenas, shouted, "You got a problem over there?"

"I can't find Barton!" Zenas yelled back. Within twenty minutes, James and Betsey joined the search. "We need some jack lights if we're going to see more than a foot in front of us," James remarked. With that, they all stopped and made several torches. They cut off an approximate nine by ten inch piece of wood from a tree, bent it into the shape of a half cylinder, and fastened a semicircular bottom to one end by strips of tough flexible bark. Then, in the center of the bottom piece, Zenas cut a hole two inches wide.

Next, he scored a stout straight staff about four feet long, which was attached at one end to the round part of the torch by punching holes and passing strips of bark through the holes. Finally, he tied the ends around the staff, which he held in his hands. With their jack lights completed, they walked for miles looking everywhere, calling Barton's name. Soon, it was midnight. Zenas looked at Betsey. Her eyelids were half closed, her shoulders slumped. "You are exhausted, Betsey. Go home and get some sleep. I'm going for more help."

"No, I wouldn't sleep anyway. I will go get David and Christine. You keep looking." The Sargent's children were now fast asleep in the Parker cabin.

"No, Betsey, James argued, you will not go up there by yourself in the dark. Robert, why don't you go?" Within minutes, Robert was in the canoe headed for the Kellers and Plumleys. Just before he got there, he began shouting, "Help, help, we need help! He saw Joel Plumley's lantern come on first. Joel was standing on his porch.

"What's all the racket out here?"

"Sorry to wake you, but a man is lost up by South Pond and we need help to find him."

"You sure the fellow is lost?"

"Yes, we've been searching for three hours. A tree might have gotten him." They all knew what that meant. By the time you were six years old, you had already known someone hurt or killed while cutting trees; it happened in Vermont as well as here.

"Okay, be right there." In the meantime, David Keller had come outside, heard the news, and rounded up David Jr. and Abram Rice. They all paddled furiously toward the Parker home.

Soon, the men and women were scattered throughout the damp woods shouting his name. The dark woods stayed silent. Zenas sat down on a stump to rest, head in hands. Suddenly, he heard a voice behind him. "Who lost?"

Zenas jumped up, turned around, pulled his gun, and stood staring into the round brown eyes of the old Indian, Captain Peter. Mitchell was with him. They had heard the commotion over the water and followed the canoes. Zenas took a breath and quickly told them the story.

"Why he cut tree?"

"I imagine for wood this winter."

"Winter wood, this way," Captain Peter remarked as he and his son began walking north. Zenas attempted to explain to the old man that he had already covered that area, but the Indian turned and continued his silent descent into the north end of the property. Zenas was amazed that from the moment Captain left, he had heard neither a branch crack nor a leaf crinkle in the silent black night.

Within ten minutes, Mitchell yelled, "He's here. He's not lost." Sure enough, he had found Barton, unconscious, pinned under a large spruce. The searchers looked like large lightning bugs skimming through the forest as they held their lanterns and rushed to the injured man's side. The men cut while Betsey, Mary, and John Plumley held lanterns. Betsey ran back to the cabin and began heating water and gathering strips of cloth. She grabbed the yarrow and garlic paste off the shelf. She would use these to cleanse the wound and stop the bleeding. Next, she gathered wood splints and whiskey from the shed. She had no idea how badly Barton was hurt, but she was ready. They brought him to the little cabin and Betsey treated him as best she could; however, unlike her husband had been, Barton was close to death. The tree had missed his torso but crushed his left leg and left arm. Betsey set the bones and treated his cuts with alcohol. Thank God, he was unconscious when she set his leg. After

46

she secured the last bandage, and Barton was resting, Betsey sat down, took a breath, and thought about how much she had changed. She could survive in these woods. She could shoot as well as any of the men, handle the boat with ease, and handle some doctoring when necessary.

However, though they saved Barton's life that night, he was never able to walk without the homemade crutches Zenas designed for him. Therefore, Zenas urged Barton to return to Vermont to live with his sister. Finally, Barton relented, and in the spring of 1838, Zenas made the trip back to Vermont. Upon his return, Barton made an appointment with a doctor. After examining his injuries, the doctor diagnosed that, with some time and exercise, Barton might recover most of the use of his leg and arm. Hearing this news, Barton said, "Zenas, I'm going back."

"What? Are you crazy? I just came all this way to bring you home!" By now, his sister was chiming in about how she did not want him there if he did not want to be there.

"But, partner, I can get better. I can work. The doc says so. This is the best news I've had in a long time!" Zenas looked at his friend and saw the passionate, lively young man all excited about coming to this new territory and settling down. Nevertheless, the land had beaten him. One slip; that was all it took. Had he not fallen in love with Sarah? Had he not gone into the woods by himself? Had he not filled up with whiskey? What if I had been there when he came home? The next morning, they were on their way back home.

"Hey Zen, look! We're almost to Newcomb. We'll be home soon, and I'll heal and be out hunting and cutting in no time."

"Sure will," Zen answered as he glanced down at Barton's leg still mangled, his foot jutting out to one side at a precarious angle. "Yup, Bart: you'll be out dancing a jig with your gal faster than a fast snow." He turned his face away so Bart could not see the shadow of skepticism he could not hide. He glanced again at the mangled foot and knew that his friend would not make it on his own in the wilderness. It would be up to Zenas to look after him, and he made a vow right then to do just that.

By the time Zenas and Barton pulled the team into Newcomb, they were hot, dirty, and arguing. Barton was mad as a cornered raccoon because one of the conditions of Zenas bringing him back was that he would not drink whiskey. He promised, but he was not happy about it. On the other hand, he knew what a friend he had in Zenas, so he aimed to keep his promise. Just as he was saying, "But Zenas, I could make enough to sell so I could help out," he heard an ear-shattering scream. Zenas yanked the horses to an abrupt halt, almost throwing Barton off the buckboard. "What!" When Barton peered over the animals, he saw the startled faces of two young women planted within two feet of the oxen. Apparently, Zenas had dozed off for a second.

"Oh, no, ladies, I am so sorry." Zenas jumped off the wagon and ran over to the two women professing his apologies. One woman wore a beautiful blue dress. The other was dressed in brown. Instead of yelling at him as he expected, the two started giggling. Zenas thought, why are they giggling? They have mud all over them. "Ladies, I am Zenas Parker, and this is my friend Barton Burlingame. We have just come from Vermont, and I am so sorry."

The girl in the blue dress spoke up, "Well, you certainly gave us a fright. My name is Rachel Dornburgh, and this is my sister, Elizabeth. We are fine. Where are you from?"

"The new settlement on the long lake," Barton spoke up this time.

"Oh yes, I've heard about that place. Not many folks living there, right."

48

"Right."

"Well, we'd best be on our way," Elizabeth chided Rachel. She was uncomfortable talking to these strange men.

"We're going to the mill, and then we'll be on our way. You say your last name is Dornburgh. Is John your father?"

"Yes."

"I know him; met him last time I was up at the mill. Maybe, I'll call on him next week."

"That would be nice. Maybe I will see you again then."

"Maybe you will." Zenas replied.

After the women left Barton teased, "Well, well, well, ain't we just the ladies' man? She sure had her eye on you."

"Naw, what would she want with the likes of me," Zenas replied, but his brown eyes followed that blue dress until it disappeared around the corner of the big white house.

Like a boomerang, the next week Zenas was back, returning each week until on one of the trips, in 1840, he returned with Rachel as his bride. She was sixteen years old, and Zenas tripped over his feet every time he opened the door and saw her. Barton had moved into his own cabin, and in the summer of 1841, Rachel announced that she was pregnant. They became family, always including Barton who continued to make and sell whiskey.

# Chapter 6

## The Town Meeting

Months rolled into years, depositing only two new people in the settlement—one, a man named David Smith from Inlet who settled northwest of his neighbors on a lake he named Smith Lake. He came alone.

During this time, Sarah Keller and her mother watched as many canoes skimmed along the water's edge, heading back to East Bay Landing never to return. Soon there was talk of forming a town even if there were only a few families. Ever the optimist, David Keller envisioned this strip of water rimmed with families. In 1836, David Keller, Joel Plumley, James Sargent, E. St John, Zenas Parker, Abram Rice, and Barton Burlingame met at St John's place. When Sarah heard about the meeting, she told Abram, "I want to go too."

"No, this is only for men," Abram told her as he reached for his jacket.

"But I live here too. Why can't I come?"

"Because you are a woman, and women can't vote. Besides, who would take care of the baby?" Abram bent down and kissed David, his first-born son, on the cheek. "That is your job, Sarah." With that, he was out the door. Sarah sat down in the cedar rocking chair her father had made for her. She reached for her basket of yarn and began knitting. Knitting always calmed her. Nine-year-old Mary Ann heard the exchange between Sarah and Abram.

"Sarah, why is it that women can hunt, fish, and chop wood for their families but they can't vote?" She was not sure what it meant, but she knew men could do it and women could not.

"I know," Sarah replied, "but that is the way it is, and we're never going to change it."

Maryann began stitching on the rag rug she had just learned how to make, "Well, I am. I vote that women go to that meeting too."

"We can't vote, Mary. Are you going to change the laws in all states? Besides, we have the children to care for." Sarah looked at her little sister. Such a scrapper, thought Sarah, though a lovely one. With her dark hair and hazel eyes, she would attract many suitors if any of them ever stayed. In a few years, Maryann would be married and have little ones of her own.

Sarah looked down at her baby and thought about Abram who was wild as a young stallion when he came to her father's house looking for work. Sarah had wanted nothing to do with him. He drank alcohol, so she stayed away from him until that lovely summer evening when the rain captured them in the upper field. They sought shelter under the Macintosh tree. Then, Abram did the unthinkable. He leaned in toward her and kissed her full on the lips. Sarah was initially stunned. She could not believe he had just kissed her. Anger followed, and she had slapped his face for the rudeness of his actions. She scurried back to the house ignoring the rain; however, later that night, lying in her cornhusk bed, she recalled that kiss. Abram apologized the next day.

"Sarah, I am sorry if I upset you, but I have loved you since we were kids."

"Then why didn't you say something instead of letting me know by kissing me in the middle of a rainstorm?"

"I don't know. My heart just took me away, you looking so pretty with your hair falling down around your face. I couldn't help it. I promise it won't happen again."

"Okay, fine. We are friends." She put out her hand. He put hers in his, pulled her over to him, kissed her on the cheek, then turned and darted off, laughing all the way to the barn.

"Abram, I do declare," Sarah chided, rubbing her cheek, utterly amused by the antics of this delightful man. Soon, Sarah succumbed to his charm, began dating him, married him, and now sat gazing at their beautiful child.

"Sarah, Sarah," Maryann interrupted. "Why can't we change it all? Besides, Catherine or I could watch David while you go to the meetings. Maryann had no idea what they did at the meetings, but she did not agree with many of the rules set for her just because she was a girl. At nine, she already knew she wasn't supposed to wear pants, drink the awful tasting stuff in Mr. Plumley's shed, have her own gun, or listen to the men talk, so she did it anyway. "I am right, Sarah, aren't I?"

Sarah agreed with her because it was just what you did when your little sister got something in her head.

Later on that night, Abram and David, stepped onto their porches, put their guns in the corner, and went off to bed. The whisper of an organized town had begun that night, and on May 4, 1837, the men held the first recorded town meeting. The town of Long Lake was born, incorporated, and governed by these men with extremely different personalities. Hence, it was not surprising that the first meeting included personality clashes and male egos bashed about. Robert Sargent and Joel Plumley wanted to be supervisor. The rest of the men wanted David Keller. He declined, due to family, farm, and cabinet business responsibilities. Robert Sargent soon realized that he could not win, so he nominated his brother, James. Hence, the election came down to James or Joel, and James won. Joel was commissioned to three slots: highways, with David Keller and David Smith, school inspector, with Barton and a man named Larson Wells, and justice of the peace, with David Keller, James Sargent, and David Smith.

At the next meeting, William Austin, who settled a half mile from St John's sawmill on a high ridge on the west side of the lake, became the new tax collector. The overseers of the poor were Zenas and Barton. Joel Plumley became moderator, and he appointed Harmon Keller the first town clerk.

As soon as the elections were over, David Smith proposed they build a road between the Plumley and Keller properties due west to his place on Smith Lake. The committee voted him down. When they subsequently approved a proposition to form a school in the abandoned log cabin between Kellers and Plumleys, David abruptly stood up and stomped out of the meeting.

# Chapter 7

## New Arrivals; New Relationships

The men and women coming into this pocket of the Canadian Shield were usually not prepared for such hardships. Many of them exited after the first winter, leaving shells of cabins for new families. Soon the two Mix brothers arrived on foot. They had nothing with them except the packs on their backs. They too almost starved to death before anyone in the community offered them food. Christine Keller invited them to dinner, and that is where Lyman Mix met Jane Ann.

On a sunny afternoon while Lyman and Jane were fishing in the bay west of the Keller farm, they thought they heard someone yelling. Scanning up and down the lake, revealed no one. However, soon the shouting became louder, followed by a shotgun blast that echoed off the mountain ledge.

"It's coming from East Bay Landing," Jane pointed.

"We'd better see if someone needs help." Lyman began paddling toward the sound. When they were within shouting distance, he called, "Who goes there?"

In a familiar voice, much to Lyman's chagrin, he heard, "It's Lysander, Lysander Hall. Is that you Uncle Lyman?"

"Oh no," groaned Lyman.

"What's wrong? Who is it?" Jane asked, completely caught off guard, wondering how Lyman knew the intruder.

"It's my dumb brother's boy. I can't believe he followed me here." "Yes, Lysander, this is Lyman." By now, the boy was in full view. Lyman set the boat ashore, and got out. "What the hell are you doing here, boy?"

"Well, papa said I couldn't stay there anymore, so I decided to find you. I sure am hungry. It's a long ways, but I did it. I found you."

"Lucky me," Lyman uttered under his breath.

"Lysander, this is Jane Ann Keller." Jane shook his hand. He had a strong, firm grip for such a young man. He was tall, tanned, handsome, and wiry.

"Sure is nice to meet such a pretty lady at the end of a dusty trip," Lysander teased. Lyman shot him a scathing glance.

"Uh, you got any sisters as pretty as you?" Lysander added, more to harass his uncle than to receive a real answer.

Lyman and Jane both laughed. "Well, mister, there are only six more of us." With that, they loaded up. Lysander and his gear, and Lyman took him to his little cabin, warning him to stay away from Jane.

By now, Sarah Plumley and Christine Keller had become friends. They gathered to quilt and make soap. Soap making was a foul smelling, arduous job relegated to women and older children. They cleaned the dried logs cut by the men, burned them, and mixed the ashes with water. Next, they boiled down the mixture in a large kettle to make potash. Then, they leached this into the water to make lye, which when combined with grease, resulted in soap.

The quilting centered in the Keller cabin, and this morning was no different. After helping Christine with the breakfast dishes, the women picked up their material and sat in rocking chairs.

"Did you see the new people yet?" Sarah Plumley asked.

"No. what new people? Did you see them?"

"No, but Joel did. He said that the man was getting on in years. There was a woman and a young girl with him, and their name is Kellogg."

Christine smiled, thinking that this would be a friend for her girls even though there was a shortage of boys.

Her friend knew what she was thinking. "I know. It's a harsh place for girls, this wilderness."

"Yes, Sarah, but it's the women that build the town."

"No, Christine, the men do all the cutting.

"But we produce the men to do the cutting."

Mrs. Plumley laughed, "Yup, we do, don't we? I do so miss back home, though, with the stores, the mills, and relatives and friends close by."

"Well, Sarah, I hope we are friends."

"Oh sure, sure, we are, Christine, I just miss home."

"Me too, but we are here now, and it doesn't do a body any good thinking about what can never be." Christine knew Sarah could be shut away in her cabin for days thinking about what used to be.

"Uh huh," and for a moment Sarah was back there in her home with the warm fires blazing holding John and rocking in her mother's rocking chair."

"So, where did the new family settle?" Christine repeated, breaking Sarah from her revelry.

"Joel thinks they already finished the house, and they are north of you where the brook empties into the lake."

"Oh, that's who's building there. A while back, Betsey and I saw a man clearing, but we never met him."

"How is Betsey?"

"Right now, with child again, but that husband of hers and his brother, Robert, are a handful. According to Betsey, they're always fighting."

"You're right about that. I also heard about another new family. They moved in across the lake from you up past the landing?"

56

Just then, nine-year-old Jeremiah Plumley and eight-year-old Harriet Keller piled through the front door all out of breath. "Hey, Ma, look outside! It's snowing hard!" They all stood in the doorway looking out at the large snowflakes coming down.

Christine remarked, "Yup and it's one of them fast snows."

"Sure is," replied Sarah, "and those new folks probably ain't got as much as a seed planted. Who would move to such a place in the middle of winter? Better to wait until spring is drawing near, so you can still sleigh in yet escape the long winter."

Jeremiah piped up, "I know them, Ma. Their name is Shaw. They dress funny and talk funny."

"Well, well, how do you know so much about them, boy?"

"We've been over there," Harriet chimed in. "There's Mr. and Mrs. Shaw and two boys. One boy's name is Robert."

"Aren't you the nosey ones, but I sure feel sorry for them, facing their first long winter in this place. Come on, Jeremiah, we'd best get home. The freeze is coming on. You'll need to bring in more wood when we get home." They quickly stepped into the canoe and paddled around the bend toward home. Sarah held her breath as the canoe bow broke through the ice skim exposing the inky black water below. This lake, a widening of the Raquette River, could be as frightening as it was beautiful. This would be the last canoe visit. Soon the ice would be thick enough to walk on, but during freeze up, it was dangerous. Throughout this period, the lake was barren except for the hapless creatures of the woods that unknowingly stepped onto the fool's ice and slid beneath it into a watery grave.

Arriving home, Sarah remarked to Jeremiah, "Well, your dad isn't going to like this. It seems people are just settling in all over the place."

"Right, Ma, they're surrounding us." Sarah knew those words. They were Joel's words now being repeated by his son, but they were accurate. A new settler named Robinson had settled on the bluff south of their land. Jeremiah had run into him that summer when he and John were at the sawmill trying to get something cut in that broken down rinky-dink place. Rachel Keller told him that this new Robinson person had already been to the Keller house and was smitten with young Christina Keller, or maybe it was the other way around. Jeremiah did not pretend to understand why the men went to the Keller house so frequently. He just knew why he went—to fish, climb trees, and hunt woodchucks with his best friend, Harriet.

# Chapter 8

## Progress, not Perfection

In September, a minister named Reverend Todd arrived. He was aghast that the people living here did not attend church. The Sunday after he landed, he conducted the first church service in a little log house covered with hemlock bark. Before Reverend Todd left, he urged the pioneers to read the sermons on Sunday. However, they responded that no one could read well enough except one man, and he cussed so much that they did not want to listen to him.

Reverend Todd traveled the same road as the Kellers because this rough path was the only way in for almost ten years. At the town meeting in 1839, David Keller, Joel Plumley, James Sargent, David Smith, Zenas Parker, and Barton Burlingame explored the possibilities of a public road. This passage would come from Newcomb and end further up the eastern side of the lake approximately two miles south of East Bay Landing. However, school building took priority for the next few years, so it was not until the town meeting of March 5, 1844, that they divided the proposed roads into three districts.

Matthew Beach and William Wood took part in the town meetings and discussions of transportation and school construction until 1837. Then, they moved south to Raquette Lake. Together with William's brother, Josiah Wood, and family, they were the first settlers in Raquette Lake.

Building roads became sporadic because planting and hunting were more pressing. The access from Crown Point to Carthage, crossing through Newcomb and Long Lake, took almost five years. The route from Nehasane area, where David Smith lived, to Long Lake was done by compass only. Progress was slow due to the many swamps and mud holes that had to be corduroyed. Corduroying entailed placing log poles close together across streams, mud holes, and swampy sections to make the road passable. The Carthage Road would become the main passageway through the town travelling from east to west. However, even by 1845, this construction was six miles from Long Lake.

At this time, an outspoken sales clerk, Amos Dean, appeared on the scene with a pamphlet titled, "An Attempt to Present the Claims of Long Lake to the Consideration of All Those who Are in Search of Good Land at a Low Price." Amos traveled the country luring people to Long Lake by telling them how the Carthage road would trail through Long Lake, and soon be followed by rapid railroad transportation. He also boasted, "Come to this wonderful town that will have access to a canal linked between Lake Champlain and the western part of the St. Lawrence. Farmers, you will have the richest soil in the territory, and property peppered with valuable iron ore."

This promise ushered in several newcomers, including John Huntley, who soon discovered the land hoax and moved on to fertile land closer to the St. Lawrence River. Zenas Parker was the agent for Amos Dean, but by 1850 only three or four new families had moved in, and the Carthage Road was at a standstill. However, that would change in 1847, when Francis Smith and George Shaw were elected road commissioners.

"Now," stated George, "we are building roads and improving what we have."

"Don't need any new roads in here. The ones we have are fine," argued Joel Plumley. They voted, and the rest of the group agreed to focus on the road construction. The men proposed building an artery starting from the northern bank of Big Brook near the western corner of William Kellogg's clearing, running south up the township line between lots 21 and 22, near Keller Bay. This would create a pathway down to Keller Bay, past David Keller's house. It would include a large bridge over Big Brook.

"But that bridge will take a lot of work," argued newcomer Francis Smith. Then, Isaac Robinson spoke up about how the road should come further south toward his property.

"Yes, but what about fixing the cow path that already runs past our house? It is barely passable," Robert Shaw argued. Soon they were all arguing, and nothing was being resolved.

"I will not be a part of this. I quit! Do whatever you want!" Francis Smith shouted above the fray. With that, he walked out, and the meeting ended, but in June, William Kellogg and David Keller Jr. joined George Shaw as road commissioners.

William Kellogg stated, "I propose that we lay out a road .3 rods wide commencing off the Newcomb Road, near the intersections of townships 20 and 21, and running northwesterly to the home of George Shaw."

David Keller Jr. agreed but added, "I think we should extend the road all the way down to the lake, ending across from dad's bay." All three of them agreed on this road, and a second one that would pass through David Keller's and Joel Plumley's properties. This pathway would commence on the new road leading from Big Brook to the lake. As Zenas was now commissioner and had a new farm south of the Robinsons' place, he proposed that the new road from Kelloggs' to Kellers' extend past the settlement to his property.

In 1849, at a special meeting, William Kellogg declared, "We need to divide these roads into districts." They divided them into four districts. District 1 comprised the town on the northwest side of the lake beginning on the road from Big Brook to Zenas Parker's, starting at the southwest boundary of the David Keller's farm, to the head of the lake.

District 2 began at the west line of town on the Carthage Road and ended at the southwest edge of Francis Smith's farm, running eastward. The Smith property was on the eastern side of the lake at the south end above Sargents' place.

District 3 began on the southwest line of Francis Smith's farm on Carthage Road and ran eastwardly on the Newcomb Road by Shaws' farm and on to the lake.

District 4 began on the northwest side of the lake and included land north of Big Brook to the clearing of Zenas Parker's farm, at the southwest boundary of David Keller's home and running northwardly to the clearing of Asa Kellogg's property.

George Shaw pointed out, "The men residing in each district will be responsible for their own roads." Later, there was a proposal to build a passage connecting to the Carthage Road. It would commence at the intersection of the Long Lake Hotel, near William Austin's new mill and house, run northward 10 degrees and on to the lake. Zenas Parker assigned four overseers to these districts—district 1, Joel Plumley; district 2, Thomas Cary; district 3, Francis Smith, and district 4, William Kellogg.

Road construction robbed the families of their men. This left the women to plant, harvest, milk the cows, sheer the sheep, and make the syrup. These chores added to their long days of cooking, sewing, hunting, fishing, child rearing, and soap making. The pioneer children were growing up. They married young and soon had children of their own. After almost ten years of isolation, others began to filter into the little community.

**Mitchell Sabattis**

**Road/path**

# Legend – 1833-1845

1) Joel & Sarah Plumley         1833
2) David & Christine Keller      1834
3) Abram Rice                     1834
4) James & Betsey Sargent       1836
5) Zenas Parker                1836
6) Barton Burlingame         1836
7) E. St. John (1$^{st}$ sawmill)     1836
8) David Smith                1838
9) William & Lois Austin        1840
10) Francis Smith             1840
11) Lyman Mix               1841
12) Lysander Hall            1841
13) Amos & Lovina Hough      1841
14) Isaac & Christine Robinson   1841
15) George & Lois Shaw         1842
16) William & Ruby Kellogg      1843
17) Peter & Livina Van Valkenburgh 1843
    (Approx.)
18) John & Sarah Dornburgh     1845
19) Thomas & Jane Cary        1845

Note:

A.    Peter & Mitchel Sabattis hunted on Long
Lake before the pioneers arrived.
B.    Matthew Beach & William Wood moved to
Raquette Lake in 1837.
C.    Joel & Sarah Plumley (2$^{nd}$ cabin)

64

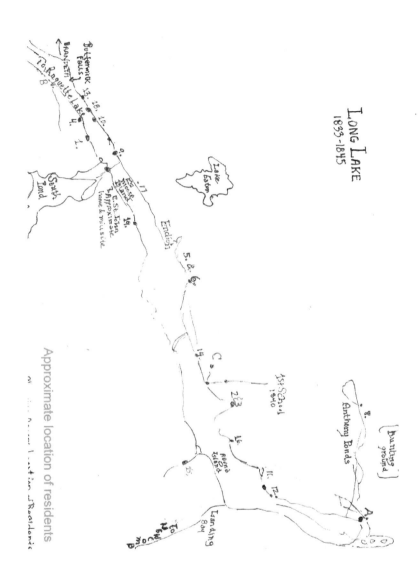

LONG LAKE
1833-1845

Approximate location of residents

65

# Chapter 9

## Jealousy and Treachery

As the winter of 1842 blew in, Betsey Sargent sat in front of her fireplace remembering another winter three years ago. All that summer, James and Robert had been at odds with each other, becoming physical when they drank whiskey. She recalled an early fall evening before the morning the two left for hunting camp. Robert had returned from fishing with Peter and Mitchell Sabattis. She could smell alcohol on him. He asked her for a cup of coffee, slumped down in the chair, and slurred, "My brother is so lucky to have you."

She knew he was harmless though this was not the first time he had taken liberties when he drank. Sometimes he would tell her how beautiful she was and how he wished he had met her first.

"Oh, Robert, that's just the whiskey talking," she scoffed as she placed the hot coffee before him. Betsey knew he would never compromise her marriage. In fact, she had become quite fond of Robert. Soon Robert began to sob as he had many times before when he was drunk, "Oh, Betsey, why did I come here? I'm never going to meet anyone. I'll be like Barton, pining away for someone I can't have until a tree falls on me and kills me, I hope."

"Lord, Robert, what rubbish. You'll find someone if that's what you want. The only reason you haven't is because you and that Hall boy are more interested in raising cane than in raising kids."

"Yup, guess you're right there, Betsey; guess you're right." Just then, James burst angrily through the door.

"What are you doing here, Robert? I told you I don't want you in here when I ain't here."

66

"I know, but I had to come home. I caught a mess of fish. Did you see them out there on the porch?"

"Yah, I saw them all right, and I hear good too. I heard you in here sweet talking Betsey, crying about how much you love her."

"James, that's not true."

"You shut up, you ain't any better than him, always feeling sorry for him, slinking up to him in your womanly ways."

"Hey, wait a minute there, James; you're crazy. She's never done anything like that, and don't talk about Betsey that way."

Betsey touched her husband's arm, "James, you are so wrong. Why do you do this?"

He pulled his arm away, "Why? Why? I know you two got something going on behind my back."

"Go sober up, James; you're an old fool," chided Robert. With that, James came after him. The coffee flew off the table, and the chair tipped over rolling them onto the floor. This was not the first fight Betsey had seen between these two. Her strategy was to leave when they started the rough stuff. She grabbed her brown wool shawl off the hook on her way out the door, gathered Mary and her son from the garden, and rushed to the lake. "Come on, we're going for a boat ride." Her daughter was used to the routine; get out of the house when dad and uncle were going at it. Betsey paddled to the middle of the lake where she could lie back and look at the tops of the trees. The fall wind bit at her face, and she wrapped her shawl tighter around her thin shoulders. They stayed until she thought it was over, knowing the mess she faced when she returned. She stayed and prayed until she thought James was asleep. Betsey paddled back in and crept through the door. All was quiet. Robert was in the lean-to and James was in the bedroom. Both had passed out. Betsey vowed that tomorrow she would ask Robert to leave.

The next morning both men came down, discussed the day ahead, grabbed their rifles, and prepared to leave for their hunting trip. Many times after these fights, the two brothers woke up acting as if nothing had happened. It baffled Betsey, but she accepted it. What she did not accept was her husband's rude behavior toward her the night before. She was cold and distant to him and still planned to ask Robert to leave. She knew she could confide in Robert, and he would make it seem like his idea to leave. If James knew Robert was leaving because Betsey asked him, he would be angry. It had to be James' or Robert's plan. James kissed her and his children, stating that he would be back in a few days. She watched them go out the door carrying their heavy backpacks and loaded guns. Betsey sat down next to the fire while Mary picked up the quilt. She could already quilt almost as well as her mother. The wind whined, the wolves howled, and the women quilted into the night. At one point, Betsey glanced over at the gun propped securely beside the door. She picked up little James and hugged him to her breast. Finally, sleep surrounded the cabin as the moon rose high over Owls Head Mountain illuminating all that lay below.

Three days passed. They spent the time canning and pulling the last of the vegetables from the garden. In a way, Betsey was glad to see the snow flurries coming. That meant that they would no longer have to smoke their meat. They could put it in pots in the snow.

On the eighth day, the door blew open and in walked James ushered by an icy cold wind. He placed his gun in the far corner, hugged his family, and ambled over to the fireplace rubbing his hands together to warm them. They were so cold he feared frostbite, but soon they warmed. He turned to Betsey and Anna, who were staring at him wonderingly. Betsey assumed Robert was out in the lean-to putting his equipment away. Betsey stared at her husband. His body was bent over as if he were carrying a heavy burden. The lines in his face were deeply edged making him look much older than his years. "Sit down, you two. I have something to tell you," he said. They sat down, and he began to tell them a story, a story about Robert that chilled Betsey to the bone and brought tears to young Mary's eyes.

James told them that after three days, Robert had gone to the west side of the lake to drive deer. James stayed on watch. That was the last time he saw his brother. After a few hours of waiting and seeing no deer, James entered the woods shouting for Robert. He backtracked and searched for his brother all of the second day. On the third day, Roberts's dog came into the hunting camp with a cut on his neck. James thought that maybe Robert had tried to kill the dog for food. When he saw the dog, he rounded up several men to help him search, but because of the heavy snow and strong wind, there was no trace of him. Betsey could not believe what she was hearing, "My goodness, James, go get Mitchell Sabattis. He will find him."

"He ain't here now. He's done his hunting and has gone home," James replied, as he ran his hands through his hair.

"Then, what about Joel Plumley? They say he's good in the woods."

"Nope, he told me that we couldn't find anything in this blizzard, and he's right; I darn near got lost myself trying to get here. That is a one hell of a blizzard out there, and I am done." With that, he stood up, went into the bedroom, and fell asleep. Betsey hugged Mary and dried her tears.

"Mary, he still may come out of this," but even Mary knew the likelihood of a positive outcome was almost nil. She knew her mother was trying to give her hope, but hope flew away in the howling wind and cracking trees. Mary understood that the chance of seeing wonderful, carefree Uncle Robert saunter through that wood-latched door was as low as the freezing temperature outside.

Winter was long and cold that year. Betsey and Mary made thick woolen mittens and tended to quilting. Visiting the Kellers or Parkers was limited due to the snow on the lake. James became more and more morose as the deadly winds rammed against the shuttered windows. Betsey tried to comfort him but to no avail. She knew he was grieving over his brother and questioning his decision to come to this wooded jungle. Some nights, he came home from chopping the new road and went straight into his room without a word. He missed his brother.

Finally spring dawned, the snow cleared, and the lake was once again full of pine bark and dugout canoes. Men, women, and children ventured out of their cabins to catch the native squaretails. Spring flew into June. David Keller Jr. and William Knowlton, a boy whose family had arrived the previous fall, were playing along the lakeshore on a large rock near the Keller property. William was chasing David around the boulder, a dangerous but exciting game they played, daring one another to get closer and closer to the edge. During one chase, while on the south side of the rock, David's foot slipped off the landing into the water hitting a rotten log. He looked down, and what he saw made him freeze in horror. He tried to yell, but no words came. David quickly pulled his foot up when he saw that the log his foot was resting on was not a log at all. It was a head! David was staring straight into a dead man's eyes. "William, William, come quick," he yelled. William came, and they both stood stark still staring at a corpse.

70

At last, coming out of his shock, William stammered, "We've got to get our dads. My God, who could it be?"

William knew exactly who it was. "It's Robert Sargent, William. He moved here right after us." The boys ran up to the Keller barn and told David's father what they had discovered. David Sr. brought the dreaded news to the Sargents.

No examination was conducted, due to the decomposition of the body. Besides, everyone knew what had happened. Robert became lost. He either froze or starved to death, not that unusual in an Adirondack winter. People searched the area, but they found nothing--not his gun, knapsack, or even a piece of clothing. James and Betsey took Robert home and buried him on the side of a hill east of the South Pond outlet.

In September of that year, Betsey entered the shed to put her dried seeds in a sack for next spring. She moved the whiskey barrel and noticed a shiny object behind the barrel. She could not move the barrel, so she reached over it placing her fingers around the shiny object. When she pulled it up and saw what it was, she was shocked. It was Robert's rifle! Immediately, she dropped it, turned, and fled out of the shed. She never mentioned it, nor handled it again.

That same month, Mary came down with the flu. Betsey could not get her fever down. Christine Keller came, and they tried everything they knew to cure her, but the beautiful blonde-haired girl took her last breath just two weeks later. They buried her next to her uncle. James was devastated. He began to abhor this horrible place that took his brother and daughter.

Reverend Todd returned that year and prayed over their graves, more for Betsey than for James. James no longer believed in prayers. He prayed to rid himself of jealousy, and he was jealous. He prayed to rid Mary of this horrible disease, and she died. James became plagued with depression, barely speaking to anyone. He spent most of his time in the woods taking dangerous sojourns in the height of winter. Betsey expected that one day he too would not return.

# Chapter 10

## Taming the Heathens

Though Mitchell Sabattis did not live in Long Lake, he did begin to spend more time there. He met a man named Palmer who was working on a plan for a more stable boat. Through their joint effort, they came up with a canoe with a square stern. Mitchell settled in Newcomb, began working on another boat that Caleb Chase had designed, and began chasing a certain Dornburgh daughter.

On Reverend Todd's second visit to Long Lake in 1842, Mitchell Sabattis met him in his new square sterned guide boat. Reverend Todd and his protégé, young Reverend Parker, watched from the landing as the strange contraption inched closer. "Hey, Mitchell, what do you have there?" Todd pointed to the boat.

"New boat; faster, better," replied Mitchell. Todd stepped into the boat gasping for breath, as he smelled the familiar whiskey stench emanating from the Indian. "I take you to the Kellers'?"

"Yes, and how is everyone?" Reverend Todd thought of the little settlement of people as his children. He had graduated from Yale and felt a keen desire to bring these uneducated setters to the Lord. He thought of himself as a savior; consequently, he was excited to see what had transpired since his first visit. He recalled that first joyous meeting the year before that took place in the Robinson dwelling on the bluff. Now, he was excited to see how many new ones had been converted. He soon discovered that nothing had transpired.

Word of the reverend's arrival spread quickly on the lake, and David Keller was down on the shoreline when they arrived.

"Hello Reverend," he shouted and waved.

"Greetings, David." Soon after Todd settled in, he approached David with his ideas. "I am here to organize a church for you. Will you help me?"

"Sure, but I don't know how many will come. Most of the men here are so busy that Sunday is just another morning for chores. You will probably get more women and children."

"Well, Sunday should be a day for praising the Lord for what is done," replied Reverend Todd.

"Yup." David Keller was not a talker, but he was willing to help Reverend Todd. Together they started the First Congregation Church with five men, six women, and eight baptized children. Reverend Todd gave his bible to David Keller before he left for East Bay Landing. On the way up the lake, Todd reiterated to Mitchell, "I believe this little town will grow as more and more farmers hear of this rich farm land." Reverend Todd recalled his lengthy counsel with James Sargent who now came to church, gave up the spirits, and was beginning to smile again. What blessings I have brought these people, Todd thought.

"Not rich land. Poor land," was Mitchell's response.

"Huh, oh, no, no, didn't you see David Keller's crops? He has a good farm."

"Uh huh," was Mitchell's response as he paddled to the landing.

"Mitchell, look in on the Reverend Parker for me, okay."

"Okay," Mitchell, responded as he paddled up to visit Zenas and the whiskey barrel. A year later, he skimmed past the church meeting place. One solitary boat graced the shore. It was David Keller's.

Before Reverend Todd's departure, he had secured living arrangements for Reverend Parker. The Sargents took him in. Betsey and the children were delighted to have a guest, especially because James seemed to respond so

74

well to him. One night, while the reverend and James were cutting wood, James asked, "So, Reverend, does the Lord forgive all sins?"

"Well, yes, I believe he does if the man is truly remorseful." James thought for a while and continued working in silence. Reverend Parker looked at the handsome man, gaunt from sorrow. He had endured two deaths so close together, but now he seemed to be eating more and coming out of his depression. He was also attending church regularly. A few more folks were staying and coming to church at the Robinson house. William Austin had built a mill closer to town that did not wash out every spring like the one St John had built. The Sargents' maple syrup business was flourishing, and five men attended the board meeting for the now legally drawn up town of Long Lake.

The Keller and Plumley children went to the log schoolhouse left vacant by disgruntled settlers who believed the wild prosperous farmland stories of land barons. Soon a new school opened at the south end of the lake below the Sargent property. The Sargent and Hough children attended it, and a man named Thomas Cary, who married Jane Dornburgh, was their teacher.

On December 27, 1842 the first white female child was born into Long Lake Her name was Livina Van Valkenburgh, daughter of Peter and Julia Ann Hough Valkenburgh. Reverend Parker was delighted to baptize the infant. The minister was quite pleased with the way the little community was growing, even though it was not fulfilling his predecessor's dreams of becoming a productive farming community. The only farmer able to survive was David Keller. The rest of the people had a couple of cows and grew enough to feed their families. This black, heavily rooted forest soil was unsuited for farming, so the pioneers who stayed mainly fended for themselves eking out a meager living for their families. Reverend Parker knew that men and women living in Long Lake were a tough breed who might not need community or religion to survive. Conversely, he knew that James Sargent needed something more. Parker understood that something was eating away at this man. He knew because he watched James isolate himself from his wife and children. Parker felt an evil presence permeating the Sargent house, and though James participated in church services, Reverend knew that this man lacked the strength to withstand what life could deal a person out here.

Reverend Parker was to experience this evil himself just two weeks later. As he approached the cabin one day after performing a marriage ceremony between David Keller Jr. and Maryann Dornburgh, he overheard Betsey say, "But, James, that is ridiculous. We would never...."

"I saw you. I saw you two together. Don't lie to me, Betsey!" James shouted. Parker knew he should leave, but if he had stepped off the porch now they would have heard him, and he did not want them to think he was listening. Obviously, James was accusing Betsey of something. The next tumble of words from James stunned Parker, stopping him in his tracks.

"Betsey, you always find someone. Now that my brother's gone, you're after the preacher." Parker could not believe what he was hearing. He was the only reverend for miles. It had to be him!

"James, you have to stop this," cried Betsey. "You have to stop this now. I was never with your brother or anybody else, and you know it!"

"I want that preacher out of my house, Betsey. I tell you he is going, or I am going!"

"James, please," Betsey pleaded as James stormed out the door and ran smack into Parker.

"Heard enough?" barked James. He continued marching toward the lake. Tom Parker followed him.

"James, stop, why I would never…."

James turned, "Right, you got them morals. Well, I got them too, and you will not covet my wife! Pack your things and get out."

"James, please calm down."

"You heard me. I want you out."

"Okay, Okay, I will, and I shall pray for you, James, because if you keep that hurt inside you, it will destroy your family." Betsey was crying. The preacher prayed with her before packing up and leaving. That night, he stayed at Zenas and Rachel's house and left town the next day. The Sargents soon followed, moving to Newcomb where Betsey gave birth to a son. A year later they moved out west leaving two ponds named after them and two mounds of earth on the side of a hill as the only evidence that a family called Sargent ever existed in Long Lake.

# Chapter 11

## The Shaws

The lonely settlement on the lake was barely sprouting. The state road from Lake Champlain was making little headway toward Long Lake, and the post office was still fifty miles away. The closest doctor was sixty miles, and the nearest decent sawmill was almost the same distance away. Because of the severe winter of 1843, many cattle had died of starvation, and the money the men were supposed to receive for working on the road had not materialized.

That first winter was almost a death sentence for the Shaws. George Shaw knew nothing about the woods. Jeremiah Plumley was right in saying they, "Talked funny." The Shaws were from Ireland. They blew in from Newcomb one stormy December day using horses owned by Peter Van Valkenburgh, now living in Newcomb. Amos Hough drove the horses. During the last leg of the journey, Charles Bissell, also from Newcomb, broke trail into the Shaws' with his oxen. The men delivered this family to an abandoned broken-down cabin on the hill east of Landing Bay and left. Charles and Peter shook their heads on the way out, betting that this family would not survive the winter

Actually, George and Robert had come earlier in October on foot to see the property. In November, they returned to Vermont to bring the rest of the family back to Newcomb. It would seem that December was a poor month to move even though it was customary to come when snow covered the ground. The snow made travel over the trails by sleigh much easier, but most people came at the end, not at the beginning, of winter. Braving the elements was a chance you took, and the Shaw family was willing to take that chance in order to escape their previous life in Vermont. The cabin was cold and damp. They made headway on patching the cabin, but soon their food supply had dwindled down to whatever they could kill including the cow they had brought for milk. Though people here lived on a prayer to make it through the winter, Mrs. Keller sent bread, and the hermit, Bowen, on the far northwest side of the lake supplied the poor folks with charcoal. Robert hooked up with David Keller Jr. and quickly learned the best hunting and ice fishing spots. However, by the time they had settled in, it was January and game was scarce. They survived the winter, and the following spring George, his fourteen-year-old son Robert, and eleven-year-old son William cleared twenty acres by hand.

After five years of poverty and hard work, the Shaws began exhibiting signs of success. That year, for the first time, they were able to load the log barn with enough hay and grain to get them safely through the winter. "We did it, sons; we'll be fine this winter." George loved his house on the hill. That year the town elected him road commissioner. Because of the remoteness of the community and the difficulty obtaining supplies, it became common practice for the road commissioner to buy needed provisions for different families and use the money earned for road labor. Those who had worked on the road could draw their pay in flour, pork, or other items. Late that summer, a shorted load came in, and though Joel Plumley had ordered a barrel of flour he received only half a barrel.

"What do you mean, I only get half a barrel? I ordered a barrel, and I'll get a barrel!"

"I'm sorry, but there is only so much to go around. We've all been cut." George explained to the irate man.

"Then you ain't doing your job right."

"My order was correct. The supplies are short. I can't do anything about that. Now, either take the flour you have or leave it. I can distribute it to others."

"Not my flour, you won't; you ain't heard the last of me, George Shaw!" he yelled as he left, slamming the door and cussing George the whole time.

In the fall of 1847, Robert and George were at the Kellogg place helping them build a bridge across Big Brook. Robert stood up to rest his back. He looked southeastward down the lake and thought he saw storm clouds rolling in. Gonna rain soon, he thought; however, within minutes, the clouds had turned into black, billowing smoke jutting profusely into the sky. "Dad, look!" he yelled pointing to the smoke. William Kellogg and George looked up and saw smoke rising up high on the horizon.

"By God, George, hate to say it, but that sure looks like your house."

"Oh Lord, that is my place. Come on, son."

"I'm coming too!" Kellogg yelled as he ran into the house, grabbed his gun, jumped in his boat, and started for the Shaws'. In the middle of the lake, between Kellers' and Plumleys', he shot two shots. Christine came out the door.

"Fire," George shouted, at the Shaws!"

Word spread through the town. Every able man, woman, and child hustled up the hill to the Shaw house. Red flames licked out from behind the trees, and black smoke filled the sky shooting out from the barn.

Mary Shaw was cooking when she first smelled the smoke. Then William came tearing through the door, "Ma, the barn. It's on fire." Mary ran out the front door, told William to stay with baby Melissa, and raced to the barn. She saw the smoke, rushed to the barn, and tried to save the few animals they had managed to buy. Mary could not get near the building. She heard the pigs squealing in the pen next to the barn. Racing to the pen, she threw open the gate and began scooting the pigs out to freedom. Just then, the whole side of the barn burst into flames, shooting embers outward in every direction. One of the embers dropped onto her right hand sleeve. Within seconds, it burst it into flames. She reacted by trying to pat it out with her left hand starting another fire on her left sleeve. By now, the cloth was gone on her right arm, and she felt searing pain as the fire burned into her flesh. At that point, she gave up trying to put it out, fell to the ground, and rolled in the mud. That saved her life, but her arms were burned. The women took Mary into the house and tended to the burns on her arms. The men threw water on the charred remains of the barn, but it was too late to save anything. The barn had burned quickly and completely. Everyone felt bad; everyone except the one person who was not there.

Lyman Mix asked the question they all were thinking, "Where in the tarnation is Joel Plumley?" They all knew the answer. William Kellogg, Lyman Mix, and William Austin had heard Joel threaten George, but no one knew his revenge would reach this level. The next day, Warren Cole, the constable, arrested Joel and brought him before the county judge. For some reason, unknown by anyone, the judge released him. Joel returned home the next day mad as a rabid dog.

George Shaw brought his little family together that night. Beneath the cloud of smoke and the stench of burned wood, he announced that they would have to give up and go back to Vermont.

"No!" Robert exclaimed. "What do we have in Vermont? They made fun of us there. Besides we still have a hog, a cow, the calves, and the house left." The horses, oxen, a cow, and the hay were gone. "I can go to work at the iron works and chop wood this winter."

"No, you can't. You're just a boy...."

"No, I'm not. I'm seventeen now, and I can do it, Papa." Therefore, after they dug up the potatoes and built a small shack for the cow, on a cold November morning, Robert began his twenty-mile walk on the long road to the Iron works, a mine several miles from Newcomb. Robert's job was cutting logs for the company. He did this every day through homesickness, knee-high snow, and long lonely walks home. Shortly, his father joined him. They did not come home every night, but when they did, they walked. George worked for one year until they were able to build a new barn and start over. Robert overcame the homesickness and was soon able to stay out there, coming home sporadically to visit his family. That spring, they had the funds to plant an ample supply of wheat, rye, and oats. They purchased a horse and an ox. They would not be one of those to go home. Living in Vermont had been a succession of insults and harassment by people who did not want foreigners living beside them. Here in Long Lake that they were foreign did not matter. All men were accepted as equals. All men voted at the town meetings.

**George & Mary Shaw**

**Robert Shaw**

# Chapter 12

## The Stantons

They came in March of 1849 in a sleigh drawn by two horses--William, Lydia, William Jr.(age five), Lavonia (age four), and George (age one). William pulled back on the reins, and they came to a halt in front of an abandoned log home situated between the Kellers and the Plumleys. Lavonia remained tucked away under a thick swath of quilts. She was sickly and had slept most of the way. When the horses' hoofs struck the ice on the east side of Long Lake, Lavonia was startled. She popped her head out from under the quilts and saw an endless field of ice with a lone log cabin straight ahead. Her father climbed off instructing the family to remain in the sleigh. He opened the door by pulling on a string, which lifted the wooden latch. Walking back to the sleigh, he pulled out the axe and shovel. "Lydia, there is a thick bed of ice on the floor. Stay here until I can chop it up, shovel it out, and get the fire going." Hacking feverishly at the ice, he began to have doubts about bringing his family here. They were tired and cold from the long journey, and Lavonia was sick. He quickly shoved those thoughts aside and finished clearing most of the ice. Then he carried in firewood from the sleigh and built a roaring fire. When he returned to gather the family, they gladly jumped off the cramped sleigh.

"Oh my Lord," Lydia whispered, shivering as she carried George through the door. It was so tiny.

"I know it's small, Lydia, but it is a start."

"Uh huh," Lydia answered, but she was not thrilled. On the other hand, William and Lavonia raced around the little cabin sliding on the ice still stuck to the floor. They immediately loved this place except for the icy wind blowing through the holes in the spaces between logs.

By the next afternoon, William had filled the holes, and Lydia had scrubbed the cabin from top to bottom.

The next day, after breakfast, Lydia and Lavonia made bread. They mixed the ingredients, kneaded the dough, and baked it in the fireplace. That evening, delicious smells of homemade bread wafted through the little home.

The following Wednesday, Christine Keller and Sarah Rice came visiting. Walking across the ice, Lavonia thought they looked like a team of horses--Christine and Sarah in the lead and the children prancing behind. William and Lavonia played in the snow with Melvina, James, and David Rice and Charlotte and Charles Keller while Christine and Sarah chatted with Lydia. "So, how many families live here?" Lydia asked

"Nine, including you," related Christine.

"Your nearest neighbors to the left are the Plumleys, added Sarah, and that…."

"They have several children," Christine interjected before Sarah could say what she wanted to about Joel. Her mother's eyes told her to remain quiet. She obeyed. "I believe one of their children is your daughter's age. I am sure Mrs. Plumley will call on you soon." They stayed a little longer and then left leaving Lydia looking forward to meeting the other neighbors.

True to Christine's words, the next day Mr. and Mrs. Plumley arrived with Harriet, Henry, Lorena, and Josephina. They were very friendly, though Lydia noticed that Mr. Plumley's deep set dark eyes dropped when she looked directly at him. The entire time he was there, except when talking, he wore a perpetual grin that made him look like he was up to no good.

"Welcome." Joel held his large calloused hand out to William. As they shook hands, Joel asked, "So what are you folks doing coming to the backwoods?"

"We plan to farm," William replied.

Joel laughed, "Guess those money grabbers got you too. This is a tough land to farm."

"I don't know. Dave Keller's farm looks good."

"Yup, guess so," Plumley replied, stood up, tipped his hat, opened the door, and walked out. Surprised by the abrupt departure, William did not know what to do, so he followed him out. Sarah Plumley had been talking with Lydia and now turned to follow her husband.

"I'm so sorry, Mrs. Stanton, but we've got to go. I will visit you soon. Welcome."

"Thank you, but who is this?" she pointed to the baby.

"Oh, this is Josephine. She was born last year." Lydia fussed over the baby until she could see Sarah was uncomfortable and needed to go. She opened the door, stood on the porch, and waved good-bye. "Please come again," she called as Sarah assembled the children.

"Come again when you can stay longer," stated William to Joel.

"Not much for visiting. Too much work to do, but there ain't only a few of us in town so imagine I'll be seeing you again."

"Ok," William replied, joining his wife in the doorway. After they left, William shook his head, "Strange, strange man, and I don't like that smirk of his." He was now worried about leaving his wife and children in this place, but he had to take the horse team back. William set up the beds, chopped a pile of wood, and brought in dried venison before he left. Lydia was now alone in this deep forest with virtual strangers. She worked hard sweeping the wood floor, cleaning windows, and making sure her family had food. While William was gone, Lydia began making red, white, and blue baskets. There were no stores within forty-five miles, and the road cut through woods was a rough wagon trail with bridges compiled of logs thrown from one bank to other.

One night after the baby was in his bed, Lydia was weaving baskets by the light of the tallow candle. Lavonia and her older brother were sitting with their backs to the window. Outside, under the window by the door, was a flat rock. When anything stepped on it, it would tip, and the rattle became audible inside the house. Lydia cringed as she heard the howling wolves up on the hill behind the house. Suddenly, she heard another sound--a rattle. She held her breath, listened again, and heard nothing. She relaxed, concluding that Madge the stray dog was probably trying to find something to eat. She heard the sound again. This time, her head shot up and she stared straight out the window into a man's face. She threw down her basket, snatched up the candle, and threw the door wide open. She did this so quickly that he had no chance of escaping before she saw him. It was Joel Plumley! He spun around and ran toward the lake. Lydia sprinted to the woodpile for the axe. This was the only weapon she had. She shut the door and fastened it with the wooden button. A chill rippled through her body. Gathering the children to her, she hustled them up the ladder to the loft. There was a small door in the gable end of the house facing the lake. Lydia opened the door and listened. Joel had gone up the lake trying to make her think it was someone else. Then she watched him make his way toward his own home. The children were frightened. She cradled them in her arms until they slept, but she did not sleep. Instead, she wrestled with mixed feelings about this place. She wondered if the next time he would kick the door in and make an entrance. She vowed that from now on William would always leave her a gun. She mused into the night at the irony of how she had thought she would need a gun against four legged animals, not two legged ones.

As Lydia was not a timid woman, the next day, she called on the Plumleys re-counting to Sarah and Joel the story about her "intruder," pretending that she did not know it was him.

"Oh my goodness," Sarah remarked, "Joel, you must keep an eye on them until William gets back."

Joel fidgeted, scuffing his boots against the floor, "Sure, sure, any problem, just yell, and I'll come over," Joel mumbled.

"Well, be careful if you do, Mr. Plumley. Make sure I know it is you because next time I'll open the door and shoot the scoundrel smack in the face," Lydia replied staring straight into Joel's dark eyes.

"Uh, uh, glad you'll have that gun there, Lydia; got to go to work now," Joel stammered as he got up and flew out the door. Lydia left soon after, and in the ensuing weeks the men and women scattered around the lake learned that Lydia Stanton was a woman to be reckoned with. They all learned but one.

Several times during William's absence, the wood-boarded fireplace ignited. Lydia threw pails of water on it to put it out, which created a smoky, ash-filled cabin.

Three weeks later, when William returned, he brought a stove. They tore the fireplace and chimney down, which gave them more living space. However, because the horse had pulled a heavy load of hay on the return trip it became sick and died. When spring bloomed, William burned over several acres of land. The whole family helped clear the land, plant, and harvest the turnips, potatoes, oats, rye, and flax. From the rye, Lydia made hats for everyone and then sold them to the other settlers. Work was hard, but land was cheap and meat was abundant. By the time winter blew out and another spring arrived, the cold December winds were forgotten, replaced by fishing, visiting friends, and watching new plants emerge from the once-frozen earth.

At this time, Long Lake Village included two little log cabins, plus a sawmill and a gristmill under one roof. When Lavonia Stanton came home from a visit to her grandparents, she and her grandfather crossed the brook that carried the mill by walking on tree trunks placed from shore to a rock in the middle of the stream and another from there to the opposite shore where William met them in a boat and paddled them up the lake to their home.

In early 1850, Lavonia and her family fished from a raft her father built for carting animals and hay across the lake. They caught squaretail fish, froze them, and sold them throughout the winter. One day, her father began clearing more land, cutting trees, and stockpiling the wood. He was preparing to erect a large frame house. One evening William told William Jr. and Lavonia, "I want you to go tomorrow and ask all men to come to my raising day after tomorrow." They were up very early the next morning, rowing through the northern part of town in the forenoon and after dinner calling on families at the southern end of the lake.

The settlement had become loosely divided into North, Central, and South divisions. The Plumleys, Kellers, Kelloggs, Shaws, Stantons, and two hermits lived toward the north end, while the Robinsons, Parkers, and a few others lived in the middle. The Houghs, Woods, Carys, and a couple others lived at the mouth the lake near the South Pond outlet. Everyone agreed to come. The house was up before midnight, and when it was finished young Josiah Houghton took off his hat and named the building, "Bald Eagle."

By the time William Stanton Jr. was ten years old, he was hunting. The men were gone much of the time, trapping, building roads, cutting timber, or gathering supplies and mail in Newcomb or Chester. Consequently, sometimes, after completing their chores, women hunted by boat at night. One night Lydia and William Jr. began hunting on the East shore across from their house. Before long they heard something splashing in the water near the shoreline. They waited. Soon they heard it amble out of the water. Suddenly a piercing scream echoed across the mountain. "It's a cat," Lydia whispered.

"Look," William whispered, as he pointed to the two gleaming yellow eyes above them a few yards away. They lit their jacks, "It's got to be a panther or a bobcat."

A dark outline emerged from the tree above them. The animal shrieked again into the night. "William," Lydia whispered. "It's a panther." Silently, she raised the muzzleloader and shot into the yellow eyes.

"You got him, Mom!" William began rowing over to where the eyes had been. There, lying below the branch the animal had been on, was the biggest bobcat they had ever seen. They took it home, skinned it, and ate it. The Stantons were here--strong, resilient, self-sufficient--and ready to do whatever it took to survive in this little town surrounded by green goliath trees, winter winds, spring flowers, and steadfast people who came for freedom in the name of no law.

**William and Lydia Stanton**

# Chapter 13

## In the Name of No Law

Unfortunately, it was not long after the Stantons moved in that Sarah Plumley became ill. She and Lydia were close friends. One blustery autumn day, Sarah called on Lydia.

"Lydia, this will be my last visit to you."

"What? What are you saying?"

"I am ill, and I had a dream. I dreamed that you and I were sitting on the edge of a large stream of water talking. We heard a heavy roaring sound, looked up, and saw a large flood coming at us. We tried to get out of the way. You escaped by climbing up a steep bank, but the water swept me away. I know it means death."

"Why, Sarah, that is poppycock; it was just a dream."

"No, no it wasn't." Sarah rose from the rocking chair and walked all around the room stopping in front of Lydia. "Lydia, I am taking my last leave, and I shall never be here again." Her prediction proved true, and in her last bedridden days, Lydia visited her quite frequently. One morning, Sarah whispered to Lydia, "Can you make Joel leave the room so I can be alone with my father? I have something to tell him" Joel only allowed visitors to see Sarah in his presence. This included Sarah's father.

"I will." Lydia motioned for Joel to follow her outside. "Joel, Sarah says you are not giving her time alone with her father. She really wants that. What is the problem?"

"Don't see as that's any of your business," he snapped and did his usual abrupt exit out the door. Sarah's father was old and he could not go up against Joel, so he never did hear what she wanted to tell him. She died shortly after, and Joel buried her on the property. Within a short time, Joel married again, burying Sarah's secret forever in the howling wind and blowing snow that trailed over the little mound of dirt facing the icy waters of the lake.

On one such wintery night when the snow was quite deep and the men were working in the lumber camp for the winter, Lydia and her sister, Mary, worked on rag rugs while the children slept. Suddenly, they heard a noise.

"What was that?" Mary whispered.

"It sounded like someone knocking on the outside wall." Then they heard footsteps. Lydia rose up, called the dog, and started for the front door.

"Are you crazy? Are you going to open that door?"

"Yes, I am. I'll let the dog get him," Lydia whispered back feeling the anger already overcoming her fear. With that, she opened the latch and let Sam out. In the darkness, she saw Sam run toward a figure standing a few yards away from the house. Then she saw the man's leg come up, and poor Sam howled in pain as the foot made its mark. Lydia quickly shut the door, draped her shawl over the window, and grabbed the gun off the wall. Mary had the bullets ready. Lydia loaded the shotgun and voiced to Mary loud enough for the intruder to hear, "Let them come in now. I am ready." The man tramped around the house making enough noise that everyone, including Lavonia now awake, could hear him. The women were so frightened that they stayed up all night.

The next morning, Mary was too scared to go to the barn and milk the cow by herself. Lydia sent Lavonia with her, and when they opened the barn door and quietly walked in, they saw something that made their blood stand still. There before them was their cow covered in blood.

"Oh my Lord," Mary screamed as she put her hand over her mouth.

Lavonia screamed, "Ma! Ma!" as she bolted out the door and ran toward the house. Mary was right behind her. "Ma, the cow; there's blood!" Lavonia gasped as she ran into the house. Lydia picked up the gun, and the three of them went out to the barn. They could not believe their eyes. Someone had cut off the cow's tail! "Who could do such a horrible thing?" Mary cried.

"Ma, it must have been that creepy thing wandering outside the cabin last night," Lavonia cried and trembled with fear. "What are we going to do? Daddy won't be home for two more weeks. He's going to get us for sure next time."

"Lavonia, you stop such talk. He will not get us because he will not get past my gun. I'm as good a shot as your Pa, or better, and I won't let anyone hurt you. Now you hurry up to the house and get the medicine rags and some fresh water in the pan."

"Okay, Mama." She turned and sprinted up the knoll. Lydia and Mary looked around the barn and house. There in the soil under the tree, where Lydia had seen the shadowy figure, were boot tracks. "Yup, just what I thought," Lydia declared.

"What? Who is it?" Mary asked, still frightened.

"It's our neighbor, Mary; not a stranger, not a bear or panther. It's a man; a man who is going to get a piece of my mind."

Lydia Stanton was not a woman to cross. She was short, round, funny, and fearless. These were the perfect traits for a woman in the wilderness left alone to fend for herself and her young. There would be a few more episodes between Joel and Lydia as the months rolled into years and the children began leaving home. The last run-in with Joel and Lydia occurred one winter morning when William Jr. went ice fishing. He walked across the lake and set his gear in front of his father's other property. Next, he cut seven or eight holes in the ice and set his hooks. Soon, William heard the familiar crunch of boot steps on the snow, looked up, and there stood Joel Plumley. William greeted him with the usual, "Good Morning." Joel did not respond. Instead, he took William's axe, reached over, grabbed his line, and cut it. He then proceeded to the next one and cut that too. William flew across the ice and into the house, breathlessly, recanting the story to his Aunt Mary.

"Never you mind," Mary responded. "I will go with you, and we will set some more hooks." They had not been there long when once again Joel appeared and drove them both home, cutting off even more lines. "You folks stay off a here, now. I better not catch you out here again!" he yelled as William and Mary hurried home. About an hour later, Lydia came home, and they told her what happened.

"Now I am going, and we'll just see if he wants to drive me away. I hope he will," she sputtered as she threw her long black sleeveless cloak around her, put on her bonnet, and took William's black snake whip from the wall and stomped down the steps. She hung the whip by her side and twisted the lash around her apron string, so she could get it quickly if she needed it.

She marched out onto the lake headed toward Joel, but before she reached him she heard his son, John, yell, "She is going. Pa; she is going!" Joel looked up, stared at Lydia for a few minutes, and then turned and walked briskly back to his house. Lydia reset Williams's lines. She was sorry Joel did not try to drive her away. If he had stooped down to cut her fishing line, she would have hit him over the head with the butt end of the whip-stock, but he was too smart, and so that day Mr. Plumley returned home unscathed.

# Chapter 14

## Tragedy and Triumph

The long winters wore on. More people were leaving than staying. The Keller women were getting married so fast that one could not keep pace with the nuptials. Mary married Lyman Mix, who was becoming a prominent man in town. He taught school, farmed, became supervisor, and in 1855 laid out the road between Lake Pleasant and Long Lake. He worked this project with William Wood, another early settler. By the time the Stantons arrived, Lyman and Maryann had two children, Alonzo and David Keller Mix.

The first teacher, Lyman's nephew, also gained a rowdy reputation. Lysander Hall was a stubborn man, and this quality could morph from a positive one to a negative one at the drop of a leaf. One day, Lysander, William Wood, John Plumley, William Austin, David Keller Jr., and Robert Shaw were staying in a camp and building a dam on Raquette Falls below Long Lake. The men had no team to haul supplies to them, so supplies were delivered to the nearest point, which could be a mile away.

"Well, we need those supplies," Robert lamented, running his fingers through his hair. "How can we get them here without a team?"

"Wait right here," Lysander replied and abruptly began running through the woods.

"Where is he going?" John asked, perplexed at Lysander's sudden departure.

Robert smiled. "Well, never mind. Let's just get back to work." They did and within thirty minutes began hearing a series of shouts.

"Come and get it. I got it this far!" They all turned, and stared at Lysander. He was shouldering a half barrel of pork weighing one hundred and sixty-five pounds on one shoulder and the remaining supplies on the other shoulder.

Another time, Lysander was in Moriah. He awoke early, walked four miles to the liquor shop, purchased a gallon of rum, and before dark had walked fifty-five miles to Long Lake. He was also known for his hot temper, gift of gab, and sarcasm. One day, while listening to a stranger who told big stories, someone suggested that Hall should tell his fish story. Without hesitation, Hall began, "It was bitter cold this day, and I was fishing off big rock at the foot of the lake. I got a bite, and I knew right away that it was a big one. Reeled it up and couldn't believe what I saw. I had caught a river trout that weighed about three pounds, and he had a pickerel inside of him partly eaten, that weighed five pounds, with six inches of the tail sticking out of his mouth."

Another night, sitting on the porch of William Austin's house, along with Isaac Robinson, John Plumley, Zenas Parker and Robert Shaw, he began, "You'll never guess what happened to me yesterday." They all looked at each other, and young John jumped in sincerely asking, "What?"

"Oh no," groaned Robert and someone else as they sat back in their chairs waiting for the latest story to come flying out of Lysander's mouth.

"Well, I was deer hunting, and I saw a dark spot in the water a mile away. I jumped into my boat, rowed toward it, and guess what?"

"What? What, Lysander?" John pried.

"Well, son, that was just the biggest bear I ever saw. Seeing me, that old bear pushed off for shore. I soon saw that this race was going to be a close one, but that old bear didn't know he was up against Lysander Hall, paddling fool of the Adirondacks. With lightning speed, I maneuvered the boat between the bear and shore. Suddenly, the bear realized he was close enough to shore to touch the bottom, so he began to trot up out of the water toward the woods. I hollered at that monster, "Oh no, you ain't getting away from me!" I high-tailed it out of the boat, pulled out my knife, and jumped on the bear's back.

"Uh, huh," Isaac murmured as he took a long puff on his pipe.

Lysander looked at him, "Really, Isaac, this ain't a story. This really happened."

"Hey, you all listening to another of Lysander's fool tales?" John Dornburgh hollered as he pulled up his boat. "For the love of Pete, I can hear him from clear out in the middle of the lake."

"Yup, he's off on the bear tale again. He's almost done though, so come on up, John," William beckoned.

"I tell you, it's not a story. So anyway, I no sooner was on that bear's back, when he up and flipped me off of him like a pesky blackfly, knocking me down on the pebbles that lined the shore with such force that it pushed the damn breath out of me."

"Well, I'm sure he didn't knock any sense into you," William laughed. They all laughed and then hemmed and hawed about how they would be listening to that one for a while.

"Hey, Lysander," Robert broke in. "Let's go out tomorrow night and find that bear and give him his just reward. Besides, we're getting low on meat. We can split it."

"You're on, Robert."

"Oh, Lord, then we gotta listen to the two of them," Zenas piped up. Soon, the men began their boat trip home to join their wives and children and either head out for the woods in the morning or begin their early morning farm chores. Far down the lake, they could still hear Robert and Lysander talking faster than they could paddle, as their voices echoed off the rock-filled mountains and gleaming black water.

Robert and Lysander were strong, ambitious, young men always looking for mischief. One day, they decided to go fishing in Canada. This time they took horses and caught a mass of pickerel.

"Hall, look at these pickerel. I never saw fish this big," Robert exclaimed.

"Me neither. Wish we had these back in Long Lake."

"Yup; me too." They fished awhile longer. Then, suddenly, Lysander shouted, "Hey, we can have them!"

Robert almost fell out of the boat, he was so startled by Lysander's sudden outburst. "What are you talking about?"

"We can have them in Long Lake. All we have to do is keep them alive and bring them back."

"What?" Then Robert understood, "Oh, I don't know. I was planning on bringing them back to the family to eat."

"Okay, let's put all mine in and half of yours." Robert agreed. They kept the fish alive, and the next evening, after landing on the shore of the Shaw property, they put the pickerels in the lake, except they were not pickerels. They were northern pike. Soon, the trout began disappearing out of Long Lake.

In contrast to these two rogues, for several months James Keller, David's nephew, had been praying for a church, "Lord, please help me bring a church to these people." The next day, a man named John LaPell walked sixty miles from Crown Point to visit. John found the settlers to be unholy hell raisers and set out to bring religion to them. Before he left, he purchased a large piece of land on the Carthage Road

"James, you are a dedicated man, but these people need a place to meet," John advised.

"I know, but how and where?"

"I don't know, but I do know that you will have your church."

With that, John got up and walked back to Crown Point. In 1855, he returned with a local preacher, Willard Austin. Soon, newly reformed Mitchell Sabattis, Robert Shaw, and James Keller set about procuring a church. They met in the schoolhouse on the Carthage Road at the top of the hill above the intersection. James and Mary Mulholland deeded one quarter of an acre to Mitchell for $25.00 for this purpose.

During this time, the settlement remained quite stagnant. There was still no post office, and few families stayed. The Kellers continued to have problems with Joel Plumley. A good cow was important at this time. It meant milk, butter for biscuits and mashed potatoes, cream, and the ability to make pancakes, pies, puddings, and custards. This particular winter had been a bad one, and a portion of the fence was down at the Keller farm. The boys were out tapping trees and boiling maple syrup, so they had not had time to fix it. Christine Keller was keeping vigilance over the cow so it did not wander off. She had seen the cow wandering around the yard all morning as she cooked, cleaned, and washed clothes on the wooden scrub board. She went out back to hang the laundry and was not out there five minutes when she heard such a racket that she thought one of the boys or her husband was hurt. She ran to the side of the house and soon witnessed Joel Plumley chasing the cow across his field bellowing, "You mangy beast, get out of my field!"

Christine hollered back after hearing several words no woman should hear, "Joel, I'll get her!" Running swiftly, she reached him in minutes. "Joel, I'm so sorry. The fence is down."

"I can see that! Fix it!"

"They're all…."

"Don't need excuses." He shook his finger in her face and spat, "Missy, you tell your husband to keep this cow off my land, or the next time it won't be coming back!"

"For God's sake, Joel, it was an accident," Christine replied feeling guilty for taking her eyes off the cow.

"Yup, and it's going to be another accident if I see it over here again because it will be dead!" he ranted as he turned and strode haughtily back through the field. Christine led Bessie back over the mangled fence, and that night the men repaired the fence.

Tragically, the following spring it happened again. This time, her daughter's wails distracted Christine from her cow watching detail. Charlotte had fallen on a rock, and by the time Christine reached her, blood was gushing out of a jagged gash on her leg. She gathered the screaming child in her arms, rushed her to the house, poured cold water on the cut, and finally managed to stop the bleeding. After tending to the wound, Christine looked out front for the old cow. She was gone! Immediately, she recalled Joel Plumley's words, "There's going to be another accident." Running outside, she searched frantically around the house, but old Bessie was not in any of her usual places. Christine called in her son, Charles, to search through the woods, but the old cow had simply vanished. Charlotte was now crying over Bessie's disappearance instead of her injured leg while Charles continued to look for the missing cow.

A few minutes later Christine heard, "Mom, mom, come, and look!" Charlotte and her mom rushed outside to where Charles was standing. He pointed to the ground. Christine looked down, dread seeping slowly through her body. There were Bessie's tracks going over the fence into Joel's yard. Christine told the children to stay there. She walked over to Joel's, marched straight up to him, and asked, "Joel, where is our cow?"

"Don't know but probably in your barn."

"Well, she came over here. Her tracks end here."

"She ain't here." Feeling defeated and guilty, Christine went home knowing her children would not have milk and butter all winter. She did not want to tell her husband that she had failed at her job but trudged to the field and told him anyway. David was not happy, but being a man of gentle nature he did not berate her or confront Joel.

That night Christine dreamed that Joel took Bessie to the edge of the woods where he was clearing land, killed her, piled logs and brush over her, and then burned her. She was so certain of her dream that the next day David went to the area she witnessed in her dream and found Bessie. Only her bones remained. Sadly, they returned from the woods feeling confused about why a person would do such a thing. Young David Jr. wanted to go over to Joel's and give him his just due. His father would not hear of it, and so once again Joel emerged from his latest escapade unscathed and unchanged. He watched them walking back from their discovery. He felt neither remorse nor sadness that they would suffer over the winter. When that thought pricked his heart, he said to himself, "I warned um. Should a listened."

# Chapter 15

## Changing Times

During the next ten years the winter winds whistled through trees and around the corners of the log cabins that circled the lake. It was a lonely time of year, listening at night to the screaming panthers and howling wolves. They had plenty of venison because the deer were easy pickings during this season. The unsuspecting animals bounded onto the lakes, ponds, and rivers, soon becoming stuck in a thick bed of ice, unable to move. During this period there was no school, except for a few weeks in the summer.

On the other hand, by 1860, Long Lake was filling up with relatives of people who were already settled. By now, most of the families were related either biologically or through marriage—David Keller, Zenas Parker, and Mitchell Sabattis married three of the Dornburgh girls originally from Newcomb. Zenas and Rachel Parker now had four children. Zenas had moved to Newcomb with Rachel but soon talked her into coming to Long Lake. They had bought and cleared fifteen acres in lot 70 on the West side of Long Lake south of Isaac Robinson. Charles Keller had married the schoolteacher next door, Martha Billings. Four of the new settlers were John and Alice Boyden, and her mother and father. They bought twenty-five acres from William Stanton, between the Stantons and the Plumleys. They built a log cabin, and planted apple trees and a garden. Joel was furious. "Why did you sell that lot? If I had known you wanted to sell, I would have bought it, William."

"I sold it to a family member, Joel. They will be fine neighbors."

"Well, if that land doesn't do me any good, it won't do anybody any good," he sneered as he walked away.

"Now, Joel, don't you go and do anything foolish; John and Alice are just starting out." Williams's words were met with silence as Joel stomped off toward his barn.

William warned John to watch out for his neighbor as he might cause him some trouble, but they worked on into fall getting the timber and lumber ready for their cabin. The hay was ready to cut and dry for winter. John stacked the hay in the corner field until the barn would be finished. Everything was ready for winter, and now John and his father would put up the house.

One day in late fall, William was going in for supper when he saw John running down the field, "William, William, it's gone!" As he got closer, William heard, "He burnt my hay! That loco Plumley burnt all my hay!" They walked up to the northwest corner where John had stacked the hay and stared dumbfounded at the black smoldering circle where the hay pile had been just the day before. "William, I can't live next to such a man," John lamented. "I would be afraid of leaving Alice alone here." He bought a piece of land on the East side of the lake, south of Watch Rock where Robert Sargent's body was found. Shortly thereafter, John and Alice built their home and soon gave birth to a son they named Orello. Four years later, they had a daughter named Olive. Lydia helped with the delivery of these two children.

The next year, on a hot August day Lavonia came home to find her mother in bed. Her grandmother was with her.

"Mom, are you sick?" Lavonia questioned, as it was rare to find her mother in bed in the daytime.

"Yes, I am, Lavonia, but come here." Lavonia walked over to the bed. Her mother lifted up the covers, and there was the tiniest baby she had ever seen. "Oh my; oh my, Mother."

"Meet Mary, Lavonia, your baby sister." Lavonia was only nine, but she immediately set to work making most of her sister's clothes, falling in love with her, and taking over the duties of her mother because the next week, William fell ill. Lydia and the boys had to snowshoe into the sugar camp and make the maple syrup that year. Lydia would take the neck yoke and buckets and gather the sap. She used troughs made by cutting small Balsam trees. Then, she cut the trunks into three-foot lengths, splitting them in two, and hewing out the middle until they would hold about ten quarts or more. She carried sap until her body ached with exhaustion. When the sun was sinking behind Owls Head Mountain, Lavonia and the baby watched their mother trudge up the steps into the house to finish the household chores, sleep, and be up at daybreak to do it all over again. By summer, William was able to work again, and Lydia was relieved.

Another settler who lived up the lake along the last sandy beach before the outlet was Ebenezer Borne, and he would come to visit. One such day, this tall blue-eyed man pulled his boat up to the Stantons.

"A good morning to you, Madam." Ebenezer, always the gentleman, tipped his hat to Lydia who was standing on the porch.

"Morning, Ebenezer, how are you today?"

"Oh, just fine, just fine, and could I interest you in a cup of tea this fine morning?" When he came to visit, he always brought his own tea. Lydia took the tea, invited him in, and began to heat the water. "Will you stay for dinner, Ebenezer?"

"That would be so kind of you," he replied as he hoisted Mary up on his lap and gave her a ride on his knee. Soon, the Plumley and Keller children came tumbling through the door to see him. They loved him because he always had something for them, such as a whistle or a slingshot.

One winter, when the snow was deeper than deep and the wind was a howling horror and most of the settler's potatoes had frozen before harvest, one defeated pioneer struggled over to Joel's cabin to ask him for a few potatoes for his family.

"No, I ain't feeding the whole town. It's your fault you didn't plant enough."

"But, Joel, you're throwing them away. What difference does it make whether we eat them or they rot?"

"Makes a difference to me," he stated as he turned and walked off, abruptly ending the conversation. He had cleaned out his barn in order to make room for hay, throwing the leftover potatoes on the ground to rot. There was no stealing them because he had two vicious dogs. Ebenezer was out in his boat and witnessed the conversation between the young man and Joel Plumley. He rowed down to his place, and the next morning several families including the Mixes and the Stantons woke up to discover a bag of potatoes on their front porches.

There was one more altercation with Joel Plumley; this time it involved his dogs. Joel's dogs had chased the Stanton's cow and oxen out on the lake. They managed to gather the animals but not before the dogs had chewed the animals up so badly that one of the oxen died. That time, Joel came down on the ice and grunted, "William, you'd better come over and get some extra hay for them animals." William was so mad; instead, he went over to the Shaws, and they gave him some of their hay.

Shortly after that, Joel got mad at Zenas Parker because Zenas wanted to build a road from the Kelloggs, past Joel's, and on southward to the Parker farm. One dark blustery night, Joel sneaked over to the Parkers' farm intending to take vengeance upon his fence. I'll show this intruder what I think of his road. This is my town, my land, and there ain't going to be no roads now or never. Hacking viciously through the timbers of Zenas's fence with his axe, he did not hear two men approaching.

"Hey, what you doing there, Joel," Lysander Hall and William Austin hollered as they approached him with their guns raised.

"No, what are you doing here?" Joel snapped back as he looked up dumbfounded to see them.

"Waiting for you to do what you're doing. Zenas hired us. He knew you would do something." Being the town constable, William handcuffed Joel and took him to the county jail. A couple of days later, William Kellogg heard of Joel's plight and offered to bail him out on the guarantee that he would vote for him at the next town meeting. Joel felt worse than a caged bobcat in jail, and he would have agreed to do anything to get out of there. He could not stay locked up another minute. He had to get back to the wind, water, and the pungent smell of his beloved forest.

"Yup, I'll do it," Joel mumbled, dropping his head down as he walked out of the jail and boarded William's wagon. When Joel arrived home, silence slapped him hard. His wife and children were humiliated. They refused to speak to him. Joel had done many things, but he had never gone to jail and left the family for weeks. Pride fell through him like an open faucet. He spent the next few years taming his temper, working his land, and becoming quite successful.

At age fourteen, Lavonia Stanton married a local man named Benjamin Emerson. They moved on to the back section of the land left by John and Alice Boyden. They began to clear the land and built a modest cabin, happy as two young lovers could be but blind to what lay before them.

106

One would think that nothing could touch this remote community and the young lovers hidden away in the crags and crevices of these domed mountains, but war has long fingers. This war was a travesty that brought brother against brother; this was the Civil War, which threatened to divide the nation. One fine fall day as Benjamin and Lavonia were finishing their harvest, they spoke of the unspoken. Lavonia had heard about the war. She knew several men who had been called to serve. "Oh, Benjamin, I hope you don't have to go."

"Now, Lavonia, I don't want to go, but I will serve my country if called." In 1862 he was called, and with tears and fears, Lavonia kissed the man she loved good-bye knowing that she might never see him again. Many nights she sat alone in their cabin on the dark backfield writing to her Benjamin. Working hard helped relieve some of her fears. One gray morning the following spring, she was digging through the dirt preparing a garden. Lavonia was struggling with the rocks, thick tough tree roots, and near impenetrable hardpan soil. She did not hear the man slowly approaching her.

"What are you doing?"

Immediately, she recognized the voice. She quickly spun around. It was old Joel Plumley. Oh no, she thought, what is he going to yell about now? She stood up and faced him. "I'm planting corn."

"Well, look here, Lavonia; you are planting those rows too close together. He took the hoe, made a few hills, and covered them. "That is the way to plant corn," he remarked. She thanked him for his kindness. He mumbled, "You're welcome, Miss," and ambled back over the field to his place. That afternoon Joel came back with his oxen. He and Lavonia's two brothers cleared the ground in front of her house and put in potatoes.

Then he left, entering his quiet, childless home. For a moment, he thought of his son, Jeremiah, who was fighting in the Civil War. He did not know if he was dead or alive. Joel lit the fire, sat down, looked out his window, and smiled as he saw the lights of the Shaw house through his window. Now, feeling the warmth of the fire and the soft light falling through the window, he realized that if this town had been only his, it would be dying with him in just a few years. The town would live. Long Lake would stay long after he was gone. And then, with one final thought his dark eyes crinkled, his mouth turned up in that crooked smirk, and he proclaimed, "I will be known forever as the first white settler to step foot in this territory."

# Chapter 16

## Homecomings

One day, as Lavonia was walking back from her parents' house, she heard someone shouting. She looked over her shoulder and saw Isaac Robinson's boat. Isaac's son, Boyden, held a man's arm, and Isaac had his bag. She turned to watch, staring straight into the young man's eyes. Oh my Lord, could it be? She shielded her eyes from the sun and stepped closer. Lavonia started running and quickly began to recognize the familiar shock of hair jutting to the right off that high forehead. "Benjamin! Benjamin, it's you, you're home!" she shouted as she ran through the field down to the shoreline, but when she drew closer, Lavonia froze, riveted in place by shock. She could not believe what she was seeing. It was her husband, but he was ghost white, gaunt, bent over, and staring vacantly somewhere beyond her head. She regained her composure, threw her arms around him, kissed him full on the lips, and then hugged him with all her strength. As she pulled away, she realized that he had not moved. She pulled back and stared straight into his vacant, motionless eyes. "Benjamin, it's me, Lavonia. Oh, Ben, what has happened to you?"

"Lavonia, I'm sorry. I just…I'm just so glad to be home, but I'm afraid I won't be much use on the farm." His eyes darted to the wooden crutches he was leaning on.

"Oh Benjamin, never you mind about that. I will take good care of you. I am so happy you are home." He could not maneuver the incline up the bank without her on one side and Isaac on the other. Later on that evening after the well-wishers had abated and they sat in front of the fire, Lavonia asked him, "Benjamin, is it terribly painful?"

"Yes, but I'm far better off than the men I left behind." That night, he told her about the Battle of the

Wilderness and how a Minnie Ball weighing more than an ounce went through his right thigh. It was not long before he was maneuvering around on one crutch, harvesting corn and potatoes, and bringing in a string of fish; however, Lavonia was forced to tackle many chores that he was unable to do.

A few months later, Jeremiah Plumley also returned home, sick and without his right thumb. While stationed in Virginia, he had accidently shot it off. Jeremiah, Benjamin, and Charlie Hanmer spent many days recuperating together and rarely speaking of the horrors they had witnessed in that devastating war. There were thirty-one heroes in all, including those who came home or immigrated to Long Lake. Among them were William Hough, Simeon and Alba Cole, George Austin, Ransom Palmer, James Bostock, Richard Parker, David and James Rice, Josiah Houghton, Alexander Stanton, Lorenzo and Alexander Town, George Wilson, Charles Hanmer, Alex Stanton, Samuel Tarbell, Walter Jennings, and Mrs. Cole.

William Wood, who had purchased land from James Sargent when he settled in Long Lake, was the only fatality. The veterans formed the Grand Army of the Republic, and through this organization Patty Wood, William's mother received a pension.

Another Civil War veteran was a young man who had lied about his age to enter the war when he was sixteen. He came from an extremely poor family in Massachusetts. As soon as he looked old enough he left the family, figuring they would have one less mouth to feed. He signed up to fight and was ushered off to Richmond, Virginia. After the war, he returned to Adams, Massachusetts, where he ran into Captain Calvin Parker. Captain Parker grew up in Williamstown, MA, which was adjacent to Adams. While visiting the area, he joined a group of men for a smoke on the porch of the general store. The captain introduced himself to the young man sitting to his right. The boy was thin and pale with brown slicked-back hair. He rocked continuously as if the rocking chair were self-propelled.

"Hello, there, I'm Calvin Parker."

The chair stopped for a moment, and the young man responded, "Good day to you, sir. My name is Walter, Walter Jennings."

"Why Walter, I heard you talking a few moments ago. You say you just came back from Richmond, but weren't you a little young to be fighting."

"Nope, not too young at all, sir," he declared as he sat up higher in the chair and puffed out his chest.

Captain Parker smiled inside. He liked this clever boy who had probably lied about his age to go to war. "So, Walter, what are your plans now?"

"Well, I just don't know. They got no work here."

"I know, but I also know where there is some work." Parker was thinking that this tough young man would be just the right fit for an area he knew in northern New York cloaked under the Canadian umbrella.

"Where's that?" Captain told him all about Long Lake. The boy left town with Captain Parker the next day. Walter Jennings spent his first night in the Adirondacks at the Aiden Lair roadhouse between Minerva and Newcomb. He walked into Long Lake with Captain Calvin Parker and secured a job as a laborer.

At the same time, John and Mary Lamos came through Newcomb to Long Lake looking for opportunities in the budding community. John built a log cabin between the lake and Shaw's dwelling. Each morning, John walked out to the pasture, checking on the animals and knowing that he would need to clear more land for them. One evening, as the sun was still peeking above the horizon shining down on the small island in front of him, an idea sprang to mind. The next day, he paddled to the island, came home, and contacted Will Hammond. He bought Round Island for $10.00 and turned it into a pasture for his animals. He brought the cows over by barge in the spring to forage all spring and summer.

One day their son, Stephen, was cutting wood when he heard the familiar rumble of wagon wheels. He dropped his axe, ran up the hill, and observed two men on horses. They stopped, stepped down, and began to walk through the woods. Stephen heard them discussing property sales. Within two months, a cabin was up and a family had moved in. By 1875, Stephen had met and married Mary Tarbell who lived in that house. Her father, Samuel, had come to Long Lake after serving in the war and settled his family on what became known as the Tarbell Hill Road. The children attended the new Lamos Corners School at the bottom of the hill.

Not all homecomings in this town preceded joyous reunions. After John and Alice Boyden had their calamity with Joel Plumley, they settled into their new dwelling on the eastern side of the lake. They were kind spiritual people who helped others in sickness and trouble. John became the first undertaker. He and Alice tended to the sick and dying without pay.

One wintery night, Alice woke up smelling smoke. She jumped out of bed screaming, "John, John, there's smoke; get the children!" John opened his eyes and dashed into the children's room. "You get the baby!" John gasped. "Come on Orello; we've got to get out of here!" He snatched him out of his bed. John turned to go out the bedroom door just as a wall of fire flamed out in front of his face. He slammed the door, turned to Alice, and shouted, "We have to go out the window!"

"No!" Alice screamed as she looked at the long drop to the ground. She was terrified but in the next instant

112

realized what she had to do. Alice held on tight to Olive and leaped out the window into the snow, followed by John and Orello. They scrambled onto a ridge, sitting silently, tearfully watching their new home burn to the ground. William and Lydia, now in their new frame house on the Newcomb Road, took them home until they could rebuild the house. Many neighbors helped with the rebuilding, and one spring day the little family settled into their new home above a small rocky island called Gull Rock. This rock was a good place to fish. One night after prayer meeting in the new church on the hill, John and Alice decided to go fishing off the rock. Soon, Alice became chilly. She draped a white scarf over her head and shoulders.

John noticed that she was cold and suggested that they go home. "We haven't had a bite anyway, and I'm getting cold too."

"Okay, Alice replied, "but see that boat over there? Let's find out what they are going to do?" John turned the boat slightly to the right when without warning, he heard a loud crack split through the evening air. Alice slumped over screaming, "My God, they've shot me!"

"Alice, Alice!" John yelled. "Oh no, no!" he cried as he dropped the oars, picked her up, and cradled her in his arms. He gently lowered her to the floor of the boat, grabbed the oars again, and began paddling swiftly back to shore. The two young guides who were in the other boat followed close behind. One guide was twenty-seven year old Cyrus Palmer. As John carried Alice out of the boat, Cyrus looked down on her and moaned, "Oh my Lord, Alice, I am so sorry. I thought you were a gull. Please, please forgive me."

Alice opened her eyes, looked into his, smiled at him, and breathed no more. It was June 5, 1872. Alice was forty-four years old. Like, Benjamin, she too had come home.

1. Manning Sutton
2. Osmond Hough
3. Viola Williams
4. David Helms
5. Frank Plumley
6. John E. Plumley
7. Jerome Wood
8. Reuben Cary
9. Cyrus Palmer
10. Benjamin & Lavonia Emerson
11. Daniel Canton
12. John Lapell
13. Charles Lapell
14. Orson Lapell
15. Nelson Cary
16. Adam Fulton
17. C. Hempstead
18. Calvin Towns
19. Lorenzo Towns
20. Mitchell Sabattis
21. Long Lake Village (Listed on map)
22. Robert Shaw
23. John Lamos
24. Wm. Bostock
25. Stephen Lamos
26. Reuben Carr
27. Henry Austin
28. Benjamin Hall
29. Joel Plumley
30. David Keller
31. Laramie Fourney
32. Orville Platt- summer resident
33. Joseph Duryea – summer resident
34. Lyman Russell
35. Jeremiah Plumley
36. Charles Sabattis
37. Lucius Henderson
38. Simeon Cole
39. Alba Cole
40. Marion Houghton
41. David Mix
42. John C. Robinson
43. Amos Robinson
44. John Rice
45. Richard Welch
46. Wm. G. Boyden
47. John H. Hinton
48. Lucius Henderson
49. Wm. Cullen
50. Wm. Stanton

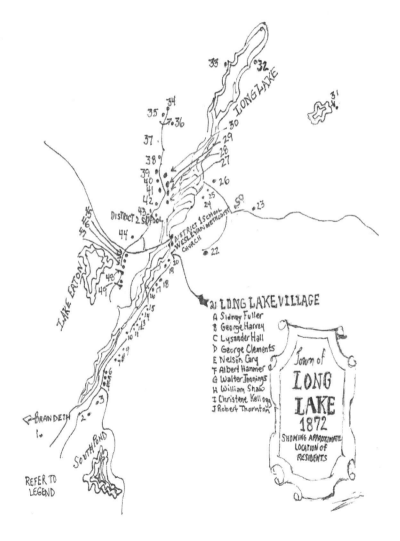

35    •32
35    34        LONG LAKE
35  •.36
37          ·30
38°        29
39         28
40         27
41
42      ·26
43    ·25
DISTRICT 2 SCHOOL   24    50   ·23
44                  DISTRICT 1 School
                    WESLEYAN METHODIST
                    CHURCH        •22

LAKE EATON

48
49

21 LONG LAKE VILLAGE
A Sidney Fuller
B George Harvey
C Lysander Hall
D George Clements
E Nelson Gary
F Albert Hanmer
G Walter Jennings
H William Shaw
I Christene Kellogg
J Robert Thornton

Town of
LONG
LAKE
1872
SHOWING APPROXIMATE
LOCATION OF
RESIDENTS

BRANDETH

SOUTH POND

REFER TO
LEGEND

# Chapter 17

## Sports Season

As dangerous and disastrous as those early years were, there was a brighter aspect brewing on the horizon. These were the early years of hotels, businesses, and Sports. "Sports" was the name coined by some of the guides for the tourists who came to hunt, fish, and relax.

Even before the outbreak of the Civil War, hotels began to spring up in Long Lake. Two of the first hotel owners were William and Rachel Helms. William was the only child of William Helms I and Wealthy Scott. They came from Scotland, settling on Lake Champlain where William piloted boats. Tragically, their new life abruptly ended when William was murdered, and his body was dumped in Lake Champlain. William II grew up, settled in Long Lake, became a trapper, married Rachel Gates, and had several children. Their home, "Wilbur's Hotel," was a two-room log cabin on Forked Lake.

One morning after Rachel had swept the older children out of the door so she could get some canning done she heard an unusual sound coming from the lake. Soon the kids came flocking in with a chorus of, "Momma, a man is on the lake playing music." With that, they grabbed Rachel's hand and rushed her past the acorn-ladened pines to the shoreline. Soon William joined them. Beautiful music pealed through the morning sun as it glistened on the calm waters. Soon, they saw the bow of a birch bark canoe floating into the clearing. Seated in the middle of it was a man with a long white beard. It was so long that it floated well out to the left as he played a large instrument, which he blew into like a horn. Trying to get a better look, Rachel put her hands over her eyes to shield them from the sun, "Is that a beard or part of the water, William?"

"Sure looks like a beard to me, but the sun may be playing tricks on us. He can play that horn though," William remarked.

Seeing the family on the shoreline, the man shouted, "Top of the morning to you folks! I must apologize. Did I wake you?"

"No, no, we have been up since dawn. Where do you hail from?" William called back.

"Oh, all about, but there is nothing more beautiful than these parts right here."

"Sure enough isn't. Where are you staying?"

"The Grand Outdoor Hotel," the man gestured as he waved his long arm out toward the woods revealing that this certainly was the longest beard William had ever seen.

"Well, come in and rest a spell. Rachel's got bacon and eggs cooking."

"Don't mind if I do. Mighty kind of you," replied the man, paddling the canoe toward them. Thus began Captain Parker's long stay at Wilbur's Hotel. He was soon entertaining folks with stories of his adventures with Kit Carson and his work with the Hudson Bay Company. On many warm summer evenings, William and Captain Parker sat out on the old wood porch entertaining the bullfrogs, black bears, and beaver with their musical serenades. William played the clarinet, and Parker played the saxophone.

By late 1850, Ezekiel Palmer, who lived in William Austin's first framed house at the southeast end of the lake on Carthage road, began taking in guests. One of his early guests was a man named Arthur F. Tait, who was a budding artist.

Tom Cary, a young man who married Jane Dornburgh, had moved to Indian Lake. They moved back in 1850 and began taking guests into their home on Forked Lake. The town flourished as more and more pioneers stayed on. Children grew up, and the old settlers became a part of the great forests, mountains, and rivers. Jeremiah Plumley, David Keller Jr., and the Shaw, Robinson, and Parker children adapted to this chiseled land cut clean by huge sheets of ice chasing giant boulders through the mountains.

By late 1860, guiding and boat building surpassed farming as the main enterprise; however, when John Keller was five years old, he was rising at dawn with his father to feed the sheep blanketing the green hills of the farm. The times had changed. Adventurers and sportsmen heard of the Adirondacks through writers such as Reverend John Todd, Joel Headly, and Reverend William Murray. After the publication of *Adventures in the Wilderness* by William Murray, who hired John Plumley to guide him through the area, Long Lake bristled with tourists looking for lodging.

Early spring brought a popular pastime that pleased young and old alike--the sugaring off parties. They boiled the sweet smelling maple syrup and piled it onto plates of pure snow. What fun it was to twirl the instantly caramelized cane around their fingers and taste that wonderful flavor. Church socials, quilting bees, and a type of baseball game were also favorite entertainments.

One enterprising young man who stood watching this new tourist phenomenon was Cyrus Kellogg, son of William. His older brothers had left while young Cyrus and his sister stayed. "Dad, I think we should rent out our house to those sports," young Cyrus suggested to his father.

"Why would you want to do that?"

"To make money. Those city people have money, and they want to spend it."

"Well, I don't want any of them in my home. Besides, I don't need the money."

118

"But I do, Father." Cyrus had been a sickly child; however, for the past twenty-seven years since he had lived in Long Lake, his health had steadily improved. Due to his illness, he had not learned how to be farmer, builder, or seasoned hunter. On the other hand, all of William's children were gifted with a healthy intellect. "We could build a hotel."

"That we could, son. Where would we build it?"

"Well, I think it needs to be on the Carthage Road and not too far from the lake. Maybe at the corner."

"And who is going to build it?"

"Me."

"You! Cyrus, you can't construct something that large. Do you have somebody to help you?"

"Yup, I have Lysander Hall, Robert Shaw, and Bill Austin."

"I heard Bill was moving away."

"He is, but he's been teaching me the trade. Besides, Dad, Robert Shaw just finished the house across the street, and it's a beauty.

After more talk and negotiations on price, William agreed to front the money. He was not a man to bet on an unsure thing, and unknown to Cyrus, William had been watching the city people flow into town too. He knew that if he were younger, he would have built the business himself.

The next week, Cyrus began work on the hotel. It was a two-story building on the east side of the intersection. The Long Lake Hotel opened its doors in 1867, and none was prouder than William Kellogg.

Just as Cyrus predicted, the people came and paid money to stay. Soon he was making money and looking for a wife. He found Christina Dornburgh, and by marrying her he found himself related to half of the town.

Soon, Long Lake was sprouting businesses from north to south and east to west. Stores popped up, along with hotels and businesses all supported by the numerous people seeking adventure. Even the guides were making money carrying these wealthy people around in their boats from hotel to hotel.

Though progress was shifting forward, one problem persisted--receiving mail in a timely fashion. Adam Fulton would leave by horse and buggy for Ticonderoga and return five days later with the mail. Consequently, depending on weather and other mishaps, it still took at least a week to receive mail if it came at all. Later, Lucius Henderson carried the mail from Long Lake to Newcomb, Aiden Lair, Minerva, and Olmstedville by horse. Eunice Helms walked three miles to the village post office during those early days. One day she received a letter informing her that her brother, Ransom Palmer, had lost an arm in the Battle of the Wilderness. She went into the small store that was in part of the hotel and remarked to Cyrus, "I declare, Cyrus, you would think in this age, one could hear about a loved one sooner than a month after the injury." She was in tears.

"Really, Eunice, is it Ransom?"

"Yes, yes it is. He has been shot and has lost his arm."

"I am sorry to hear that. This war is Hell. I agree with you about the mail." Later on that night, he began to think about Eunice. Why couldn't I have a post office at my hotel? "Christine, what do you think about having the mail delivered to the hotel and people coming here to pick it up?" Christine agreed, and so the first post office began with Cyrus holding the postmaster position for thirteen years and Christine doing the job.

In the meantime, Lavonia and Benjamin Emerson opened a boarding house a few miles south of the Long Lake Hotel.

Even Mitchell Sabattis joined in the fray, building The "Mitchell Sabattis House and Garden," approximately one quarter of a mile from the Long Lake Hotel. Cyrus Kellogg's youngest daughter, Harriet, who was eleven when she came to Long Lake, married Ezekiel Palmer and ran a hotel, The Palmer House, south of the Sabattis House on the Carthage Road.

In 1878, Cyrus approached Henry Austin with a proposal. "I'll tell you what, Henry; I know you have wanted to buy this hotel for some time. I would like to sell it to you now."

"Uh huh, and what are you asking for it?" Henry knew the Kelloggs, and he knew they did not miss a turn to earn a dollar so he expected a high price.

"Well that depends."

"Depends on what?"

"On whether you have the money to buy it and if you are willing to help me build a new business."

"A new business!" "Where?"

"Down the road on the lake next to the pond."

"You're joshing me."

"Nope, I'm serious."

"Why would you want to build there? That ain't no pond. It's a swamp."

"I have my reasons. My price is low for this place, and I have Christine's brother out of Newcomb who will build the new hotel, but he needs help."

Two months later, Cyrus turned the Long Lake Hotel over to Henry Austin. However, Henry rented rather than bought it, and in 1878, Cyrus and Christine Kellogg opened the Lake House, a three-story structure on the east shore facing the lake. They rented rooms and ran a store.

Cyrus knew that tourists were paying big money to see raw nature. Raw nature faced the bedroom windows of the hotel. Raw nature was Long Lake, and soon the hotel was booming as well as the blacksmith shops, Houghton's store, Murray's Store, and the harness shops. The sawmills continued buzzing as more people moved in and built houses. Sadly, some of the tough old timers were breathing their last.

One morning almost one year to the month of the Lake House opening, Christine Kellogg woke up, turned over to wake Cyrus, and discovered that he had died in the night. She was all alone and scared. She notified Stephen Lamos, now undertaker, and he and his young son, Morris, handled the funeral. Christine immediately sent word to her sons who had moved away. She also sent word to her brothers asking them to come home and help with the hotel. They refused. She buried Cyrus, finished her crying, put her shoulders back, and marched into the hotel running it until 1893 when she sold it at a good price. She discovered that Cyrus was not the only business-minded one in the family.

Henry Austin continued to operate the Long Lake Hotel for several years. One day Henry's son, David, came to him with a request similar to the one Cyrus had brought to his father.

"Dad, I'd like to start my own business. I'd like to own a hotel," David articulated.

"You know you would be in direct competition with me, don't you?"

"But dad, there are so many tourists now that we are filled to capacity every summer night."

"Where would you build it?"

"Down in the grove. That way I would catch people coming in from the south.

"Sounds like a good plan, son." David went on to construct and open the boarding house, which was filled every night. He called it The Grove. He catered to sportsmen and worked with guides such as John and Jerry Plumley, Amos Hough, Henry Stanton, the Robinson men, Sabattis men, Reuben Cary, and Alonzo Wood. Many nights, these men would gather around the fire and talk about their hunt. There were stories and competitions based on who bagged the largest moose or deer or whose clients caught the biggest fish. Henry usually traversed the lake in one of the latest hand-crafted boats. He named his newest creation the Adirondack Guideboat.

A few years later, Henry Austin turned over the Long Lake Hotel to William Helms and Theron Smith.

**John Helms with father, Bill Helms**

**The Long Lake Hotel (Hoss's Country Corner)**

**The Grove House-1887**

**The Grove House, 1888**

**The Kellogg Lake House, 1878**
**(Hotel Adirondack)**

**The Kellogg Lake House under construction after it burned (1903)**

# Chapter 18

## The Sagamore and the Buttercup

In the winter of 1881-1882, William Dornburgh began playing with the idea of building a grand summer hotel on the lakeshore. He went to see Mitchell Sabattis.

"Mitchell, would you be willing to sell me a section of your land so I can build a hotel?"

Mitchell thought for a moment. Because he no longer drank, he had become quite successful, acquiring a large amount of shoreline stretching from his lodge, northwest, to a point across the water from the Kellogg Lake House. "What's your price and what part?"

"I'll give you five hundred dollars for thirty acres of that piece southwest of you that projects out into the lake."

"Show me," replied Mitchell. They walked the perimeter of the property, discussed it, and Mitchell agreed to sell. Henry Kellogg surveyed the section, and lumberman, Edmund Butler Jr. of Minerva agreed to help with the financing. William immediately began construction, and the whole town came out to watch the progress. It was slated to be the largest building in Long Lake. The finished mansion was a remarkable sight, and nowhere in the Adirondacks had a more spectacular hotel. Soon people flocked to Long Lake to enjoy the lake, beach, parties, and the luxury of the Sagamore Hotel.

It was not long before all this commotion attracted the attention of some very wealthy investors, one being the son of Dr. William Durant, the famous railroad tycoon. William wanted an appropriation of $1,000 from the Town of Long Lake to build a carry from Forked Lake to Long Lake. The Durants owned the Adirondack Company Railroad running from Saratoga to North Creek. Passengers journeyed further by overland travel, then by steamboat up river to a three-quarter of a mile ride on the Marion River Railroad and again by steamer up the Eckford Chain of Lakes to Raquette Lake. They would then connect with steamers on Forked and Long Lake. It was a well thought out plan; however, when the Long Lake guides who earned their living by paddling tourists up the lake to the various businesses heard about it, they were angry. This plan would replace them, and Durant already had their replacement built and ready to go. It was a steamboat called The Buttercup.

At the annual town meeting of 1884, Durant put forth a proposal that for a mere stipend of $1,000.00, Long Lake could have a steamboat bringing tourists into their town. This would increase business ten-fold. Durant was sure the people would be as positive about the endeavor as he was.

"And what are us guides supposed to do while your steamboats are cruising down the lake sucking up our business?" piped up Charlie Sabattis, Mitchell's son.

"Times are changing," remarked Durant.

"By way of your presentation, I understand you already have this boat built and ready to go," stated Robert Shaw.

"That's right. I'm putting her in on Monday."

"You can't do that," said Maryann Keller, who was sitting next to her brother. Maryann had walked into her first meeting five years ago. No one knew she planned to attend, not even her brother. Maryann walked in, sat down, and amazingly, not one man spoke up. However, after the meeting there was a heated discussion with her brothers about her attendance. She saw them standing in a circle and knew it had to be about her, so she marched over to the men and stated, "I live in this town too. I can't legally vote, but there are no laws stating that I can't attend the public meetings. I run a business just like the rest of you. I am not married, so I have no representative; therefore, I'm coming to the meetings. Maryann was the only tailor in town, so these men knew her well. She made their Sunday best suits. She said her piece, turned, and ambled on home. At the next meeting, the men greeted her and business went on as usual. After a couple of years, she was joining in the rhetoric just like the men, and this past year, her nephew's wife, Pauline Houghton Rice, had begun attending with her husband, James.

William Durant responded to Maryann's comment with, "Why not, and who are you?"

"Because we ain't said so," Lysander Hall butted in.

"I am Maryann Keller, and I can tell you right now that the guides won't approve your plan.

"Uh, right, Missy, but folks, listen here, I'm just here out of respect. I don't need your money to do this."

"But you do need our vote," Lyman Russell replied.

"Maybe."

"Well, maybe we just need to put it to a vote," Warren Cole managed to interject as he visualized his boat building and guide business swept away under the wake of the enormous steamboats saturating Long Lake. After much more clamor, the resolution was voted on and turned down. Durant stormed out more determined than ever to do exactly what he wanted to do, and he did. He was so convinced that once the boat was in operation, the people would see how beneficial it was and come around to his way of thinking. Within a couple of days, he ordered his men to construct a dam at Raquette Falls, six miles downriver from the foot of Long Lake. Soon, much to the people's chagrin, The Buttercup was moored at the Sagamore Hotel and running tourists up and down the lake. The guides hollered about it at town meetings, Bill Hanmer's Store, the local barbershop, and each other's porches. Young Durant failed to consider that these pioneers had fought through hard winters and mud soaked springs to feed their families, and no rich city man was going to take it away from them.

Lysander, now sixty-one years old and somewhat subdued, was still headstrong. Every time he saw that steamboat skimming down the lake, he seethed inside, as did Wallace, Jeremiah, and John Plumley, Charles Hanmer, Edwin Stanton, Charlie LaPell (John and Livinia LaPell's son), Farrand Austin, and all the other guides. One night, Lysander confided to his wife, Harriet, "That Durant can't get away with taking money right out of our pockets."

"Well, I don't see that there is much you can do about it, Lysander," replied Harriet.

"I sure as hell can and intend to."

"Now, Lysander, don't you go doing anything foolish. You're not a young buck anymore." She knew her husband. He didn't have a fearful bone in his body, and once he got an idea in his head, there was no getting it out. That night, Lysander secretly met with Charlie LaPell, Wallace Plumley (John Plumley's son), and several other men he knew he could trust.

"Okay, men, I think we need to make that steamboat disappear."

"Sure as hell do," snapped Charlie, knowing his father would raise cane with him if he knew what he was getting ready to do.

"Well, I got a plan, but it ain't gonna be pretty, and if we do it, we got to swear to secrecy."

"Don't care about pretty; I care about making a living," Wallace quipped back.

"Okay, but I gotta have your word before I tell you. You're either in or out. If you're out, you need to leave now."

These men had grown up with Lysander. He had matured from a wild kid to a man they looked up to. They

130

all pledged to secrecy. Lysander began, "First, we need to dynamite the dam that fool built at the foot of the lake."

One of the men jumped in, "But, what about the watchman? Durant's got a night watchman down there watching that dam."

"Got that figured out. Our best shooter in the group will fire a shot into the watchman's campfire." They all knew who that expert shot was, and they all turned and looked at the dark haired, dark skinned man leaning against the tree. He nodded his head. "That will send the watchman running for help while we steal the boat, and you others blow up the dam. The guard will run to Johnson's Lodge for help. That is a full two miles from the dam. That gives you time to do it and get out. The dark haired man's brown eyes gleamed in the night air, and he replied gruffly, "You got it. I'll do my part."

"Right!" Next, Charlie, you and I will paddle our guide boats up to the Sagamore where the Buttercup is moored. Wallace, you will ride with me and then board the Buttercup. While we are dragging the boat out to the middle of the lake, you will cut holes in the hull with your axe. When you finish, you will return to my boat."

"Got it." The men dispersed that night with a solid plan and the date to execute it.

That evening as Wallace walked his girlfriend, Annie Scott, home, she sensed that something was wrong. He was unusually quiet and tight-lipped. "What are you up to, Wallace? I know that look."

"Oh, just had a meeting with the men."

"What men?"

"Oh, some other guides."

"Like your father and your Uncle Frank?"

"Can't say."

"Oh." She thought a moment. "Okay, when are you doing this?" They had discussed the financial ramifications

131

of the steamboats, and Wallace had threatened that the men would take some kind of action. She figured that was the topic of the meeting.

"In the spring. That is all I can say, Annie"

"Okay."

"Except that Durant shouldn't mess with us."

They hugged at Annie's cabin, and she watched Wallace walk out the door. Oh, good Lord, please don't let him get hurt, she thought to herself.

That same night, young Lyman Russell talked to his wife, Angie, about his concern over the welfare of his work. "Angie, if this rich man, Durant, comes in here and puts steamships on the lake, I don't know how we will survive." He looked down at his young daughter, Hattie, gulping down the last bit of potatoes on her plate.

"Oh, Lyman, we will be fine. We will be fine." She patted him on the shoulder and began gathering up their few dishes. She knew from her brother, Henry Henderson, that the guides were furious at the thought of losing their livelihood. It frightened her too.

It happened the following June on a warm evening. All went as planned. The guard, frightened by the gunfire, did race to Mother Johnson's Lodge. Halfway there, he heard a loud explosion. The next morning, in the silence of the dawn, Jerome Wood, pilot of the Buttercup, discovered that it had vanished from the Sagamore. The constable feigned investigation, the town board feigned interest when Durant came demanding justice and threatening to put an even bigger boat on Long Lake, but it would be ten years before another boat of that size graced the shores of Long Lake. The men who did it never told. The town folks secretly knew and never told. Besides the guides, the only people who knew for sure were Harriet Hall, Sadie LaPell, and Annie Plumley until they told their best friend, Angie.

The Old Sagamore Hotel

Sagamore Beach & Guideboats, 1880

**Rear center: Mitchell Sabattis & John Keller.
Front center, Farrand Austin and sports**

**Harriet Hall**          **Lysander Hall**

# Chapter 19

## The Brothel and the Preacher

As the news spread about the Buttercup incident, tourists began to question the safety of coming to such a treacherous place. In addition, now their only transportation was the crude but beautiful guide boat. This added to the financial problems brewing at the new Sagamore Hotel. The original owner did not have the money to run the hotel, so it fell back on Edmund Butler to take over the reins. When he realized that he could not recoup his losses on the hotel, he began opening the doors to another more profitable business. This elite beacon on the lake soon became an embarrassment to the town and churches in Long Lake, especially the Wesleyan church and especially Robert Shaw who was the supervisor. In addition, the men had made a deal with Butler, which resulted in the Sagamore providing space on the first floor for their monthly meetings. Reverend Shaw approached Butler about the matter. He began with, "Mr. Butler, this town is noted for its good reputation. We will not have an establishment the likes of this in Long Lake. Please stop bringing in these unholy women."

"What?" questioned Butler, feigning shock at the accusation, "I beg your pardon? My servers are not unholy. How would you even presume to know that?"

"Servers! Mr. Butler, you and I both know that these girls are not servers."

"Why Reverend, I have no idea what you are talking about. Of course, they are. What else would they be?" Butler chuckled, silently baiting the reverend to use the word prostitute. He knew there was no proof, and he did not care what Shaw thought.

"Ed, we are trying to build a family community here, and we cannot have these goings on at the Sagamore. We are getting reports of loud parties and drunkards falling into the lake."

"Reverend, I guarantee you that there is nothing going on here to tarnish Long Lake's reputation, and I will try to keep the employees in line," Butler reassured Shaw as he ushered him out the door. As soon as Shaw left, Butler told his workers, "I told that minister a good story, so you boys keep quiet and no more wild parties in the bar for a while." However, these men were not the kind who listened to anyone. One night in 1889, several of the men employed to work on the new bridge in town had too much to drink and commenced to get into a huge brawl. During the fight, they knocked down a lantern. Flames immediately sprang up. That night, the hotel burned to the ground. It was only four years old. Desperate for help, at the following monthly meeting Butler approached the people for money to help rebuild.

"Folks, I only need $12,000, and I could rebuild. It is just as good for Long Lake as it is for me personally."

"Not so high and mighty now," Robert Shaw chimed in remembering his visit and the lies Butler told him.

"I told you the truth, Robert. You were wrong about a brothel, and I had a legal right to serve alcohol"

"Except when it caused a place to go up in flames," Willard Sutton chided.

"And except when half naked men and women are running out the doors with sheets wrapped around them," mocked John Plumley. The men began to murmur among themselves remembering that frightful night when the Sagamore Hotel's flames licked the night sky and lit up the whole town.

Edmund heard this, saw the way it was going, and quickly spoke up, "Folks, let's just table this, and you go home and think about it for a while." They voted to table it for two weeks. Butler knew several of these men on the board, and he had a plan. The next day, he drew up a petition, contacting each voter and promising them money or other favors if they signed his petition to fund the rebuilding of the Sagamore. Boyden Robinson was for it because Butler offered him money for a circular saw for his mill, and promised that he would throw business his way for the purchase of construction materials. The Bissells, who owned Centennial House southwest of the Sagamore, voted against it because their business had increased since the hotel fire. Orin LaPell and Stephen Lamos, who now owned a sawmill and shingle mill, signed the petition because their business had dropped since the fire. As with their ancestors before them, these men had to prioritize providing for their family. They saw the new hotel as insurance for the survival of the town. The next part of Butler's plan involved meeting Mr. Shaw late one night in the freight room of Robert's store.

"And to what do I owe this visit?" asked Shaw.

"I have come to ask for your vote on the issue of rebuilding the hotel. If you do that, I will guarantee that all of my guests will come to your store and your store only to purchase supplies.

"Well, Mr. Butler, I am amused. I will say to you right now that you cannot stir me with offers of any kind."

"That may be, but others have already signed a petition to go with my plan, so I would suggest you do the same. The rest of the board is against you."

Because the settlement was so small, Robert already knew about the petition, but he acted surprised. "My, my Mr. Butler, I see you have been busy. Let me have twenty-four hours to investigate, then meet me back here, and I

137

will tell you whether I will concede or not. He went to each person Butler mentioned, and asked if he had signed the petition. The majority of them had signed it. Later on, he met with his brother, William, who told him that the people were blaming him for not having a grand hotel in town. He suggested that Robert go along with it and let them learn from their own mistakes. Next, he met with John LaPell, the most spiritual man he knew. He advised him to walk away from the matter, so that evening Robert met with Ed Butler and told him, "Ed, this is the first time I have ever taken my hands off an undertaking, but I am afraid for my sanity. I am against the whole idea, but since Supervisor Boyden has also signed the petition, I will step down and vote to give you the money. I want to state to you that I am opposed to it, but I will not be the only man to stop it."

Mr. Butler, visibly moved by Robert's words, offered Shaw his hand, thanking him for his kindness. The next day, the Town of Long Lake gave Edmund Butler the money. Months went by, and the $12,000 was spent; however, the hotel was not completed. Because Ed Butler had no credibility, he could not get the funds to complete it. The town was now out $12,000 and still had no hotel. Butler became physically sick over it and thought he was dying. One Sunday after church, Robert went to visit him. Edmund was surprised but thanked him for coming. A few weeks later, Butler asked to see Robert again. This time he told him what was going on. He confessed that he could not finish the hotel and had given up hope of ever getting the money to complete it.

"Well, really, that is too bad. There is so much money in the country it seems as though you ought to find enough to complete this house, replied Robert. I will see what I can do to help you, if you like."

Butler was stunned to think that this man would offer to help him. "Why, thank you, Robert, I am in your debt."

"No, I do this not only for you, but for our town. I have come to believe that we need the hotel, but you are not in my debt."

True to his word, Robert travelled from New York City to Plattsburgh trying to procure financing, but no one would entrust the money to Butler. Hesitantly, he had to come home and tell Ed that he could not get the funds. Mr. Butler took to his bed again, becoming worse each day. One morning he awoke and remembered another investor he had forgotten about. He summoned Robert again and asked him one more time to go to New York City. The next day Robert left for the city, once again travelling over rough roads and finally arriving at the potential investor's home. After waiting for hours, he was ushered in to see a Mr. Hoe. Robert told him of the investment opportunity, which he knew was a long shot. Who would want to invest in a hotel in some out of the way place called Long Lake, forty-two miles from a railroad? He explained the situation to Mr. Hoe.

"And who am I giving this to, please?" asked Mr. Hoe.

"Mr. Edmund Butler."

"I do not care for Mr. Butler."

"Then do it for me." Mr. Hoe agreed to the deal, but only if Mr. Shaw would receive the check for five thousand, and when Edmund had spent that Hoe would send Robert another check. Shaw returned with the good news, and within a few days Butler was out of bed organizing the continued construction of the new hotel. When it was finished, the Sagamore Hotel stood five stories high, one hundred and twelve feet long, fifty feet wide, and commanded a glorious view of the lake. It was the most magnificent structure in the Adirondacks. Sadly, Edmund Butler never did recover financially; however, he and Robert Shaw remained lifelong friends.

# Chapter 20

## Relationships

By 1899, a railroad station sprang up only nineteen miles from Long Lake and was known as Webbs' Railroad. This resulted in several new camps populating the lake. People such as Dr. Cottrell, Howard Stephens, Dr. Woodard, George Terry, Senator O.H. Platt, Dr. Duryea, and the Harpers owned these new luxury homes. The Sagamore catered to these elites. The little town was growing. The Houghton, Shaw, and Cole stores were booming. On Pine Island, across from the Lake House and the Sagamore, folks came out in the early evening to hear Calvin Parker's band. Members of his band included Isaac Sabattis, David Mix, Boyden Robinson, and William Kellogg. The Wesleyan Church hosted picnics at the Sagamore, and the guests played croquet and tennis. Tourists languished in the afternoon sun boating and swimming in the clear blue lake waters. Even farmers such as David Keller and newcomer John (Ransom) Seaman joined in the prosperity by selling fresh produce to the hotels and restaurants. Friendly rivalry among rowers of the town often led to an impromptu race.

Though Caleb Chase and Mitchell Sabattis had been building guideboats for some time in Newcomb, now men such as Reuben Cary, Henry Stanton, Isaac Sabattis, and Orello Boyden began building them in Long Lake. Vet (Sylvester) Cole, twin of Clayton, had taken on the task of delivering mail to Blue Mountain Lake, and the highway between Helm's, Grove Hotel, and Blue Mountain Lake was completed.

James Bissell, Lena Bissell, and Andrew Fisher from Newcomb, who owned The Centennial on the west side of the lake about a mile south of the bridge, continued to expand the building. James was an accomplished carpenter and cabinetmaker. Andrew was a builder. The original hotel building was in the Queen Anne style.

**Endion, The main house, 1893**

In 1894, Lena met a man named Frederick Remington who told stories about canoeing through Canada. On one of his canoe trips, he heard an Indian say the word, "Endion." Curious, he asked what it meant in English. The Indian told him that it meant, "Home." Lena liked the word so much that she renamed the hotel Endion. Hence, the road into the lodge became Endion Road. They built a ferry and soon the barge-like contraption was seen carrying passengers across the lake alongside George Smith's steamboats, <u>The Iris</u> and <u>The Daniel P.</u>

Lena's neighbor was Clayton Cole. Several times during the years, he would set fire to his blueberry fields, which was common practice; however, his fires were larger than most. Several times, he and James had words about the threatening fires. One such time, in 1898, after one of Clayton's fires, Lena charged over and banged on his door. He came to the door, opened it, and greeted her with, "Lena, what is the problem today?"

"Clayton, you know what the problem is. Come with me."

"Don't think I can right now. State your business."

"That last fire you set came within five feet of our property, and there are still some live embers over there. She pointed toward her property. Finally, Clayton came out and followed her. They walked over a fiddle fern-laden knoll and half way down a blackened bank Lena pointed, "See the smoke?"

"Yup, I see it, Lena." He walked over and stomped the wet leaves down with his boots. The circle of smoke died down, but Lena was still worried. "Clayton, this is your problem and mine. One day you're going to burn us all down!"

"No, I ain't. Besides I gotta burn, so I can replant."

"You don't have to burn that much. My blueberries are fine, and I don't set fire to all of them at once. It is just too dangerous."

"Uh huh, well then, I suppose we'll have this neighborly visit every year because this is my land, and I'm going to farm it the way I see fit."

Lena was fuming, "Oh, you are such a stubborn man!" She turned and stomped back through the woods to her house. Later that night, Lena and James talked. The next spring, they offered Clarence a tidy sum for his property. He sold it and moved on to terrorize someone else with his blueberry fires.

Relationships among church folks did not fare much better than relationships among secular neighbors. Throughout this period, several people were banished from the Wesleyan church for such evil deeds as drinking alcohol, cussing, or missing church. Jeremiah Plumley and his sister Harriet Plumley Henderson were kicked out for swearing. Andrew Mulholland, much to his wife Christine Keller's chagrin, was banished for drinking alcohol. Many people were put on trial, found guilty, and then allowed to come back in under a sworn oath that they would not sin again. This created division among some folks, culminating in the idea of building another church. Several people of the Catholic faith had settled in Long Lake but had to travel quite far to attend church. Therefore, many people were meeting in their homes. In 1899, on a little knoll, beside the Union Free School, Andrew Fisher built a Catholic Church. The church accommodated all the locals in the winter and swelled to capacity in the summer.

With the coming of steamboats on the lake, the demand for guides lessened; however, guiding did linger on due in part to the formation of the guides association in 1892. Verplank Colvin, a topographical engineer who first surveyed the Adirondacks, led the meeting. The guides implemented a system that brought the employer and employee together, often in lasting friendships. Among those from Long Lake at the second annual meeting were Farrand Austin, Cyrus Palmer, Charles and Clayton Cole, Wallace and William Plumley, William Cullen, William and Isaac Robinson, David Hough, David and William Mix, Lyman Russell, Edwin Stanton, and Willard Sutton.

In order to accommodate the steamboats and the increasing population, people had to look at the old structures put in place many years before. One structure, the float bridge, was rotting and hazardous, but the town refused to appropriate money to build a new one. After several accidents on the bridge, and Isaac Robinson sued the town because his horse fell through it and drowned, they shut the structure down, and Frank Burch ran a ferry across the lake. Finally, the town voted to fund a new bridge, which was completed in 1901. Timothy D. Sullivan was supervisor, and the span consisted of two bridges—a short one to Pine Island and a larger one from Pine Island to the west shore. The town moved the previous smaller bridge to the Raquette Lake outlet on North Point Road. All of these improvements added to the prosperity of the little town as it spread its wings into late 1800, and young people began meeting others from outlying areas.

One such meeting took place between Annie Hodgson and Jerome Wood. One day in an umbrella manufacturing plant in Sheffield, England, Annie Hodgson wrote her name and address on the inside of an umbrella she had just completed. "Why are you doing that?" her co-worker Ruth asked.

"Oh, I don't know. It is like the message in the bottle. Who knows? One day my prince charming may purchase it and come here to sweep me off my feet."

"You are a dreamer, Annie, and you better hope Mr. Fisher doesn't see that or you will be dreaming about getting a new job."

"Oh, you worry too much," Annie retorted and continued with her work. A few months later, she received a letter from Jerome Woods of Long Lake, New York, stating that he had purchased her umbrella. The next day, Annie brought the letter to work and showed Ruth, "Ruth, I can't believe it. I received this letter from a man in the United States. See, now what do you say? Am I a dreamer?"

"Well, my goodness, you don't know anything about this American. He could be a scoundrel."

"True, true, but he wrote," Annie replied holding the letter to her heart and twirling around in circles." Jerome continued to write to Annie until in 1887, then she came to the United States to work as a housekeeper for her brother who resided in Troy. Later, she travelled to Palmer's Falls in Raquette Lake, where she found employment at The Antlers. Jerome worked on the lake for William Durant. Soon, the two met, fell in love, and married.

It would seem as though at this point in the history, the town continued to grow and prosper. It did not. One profession of most importance to a small town with few passable roads in or out was the town doctor. Long Lake had no doctor, and the pioneers would pay dearly for that oversight.

# Chapter 21

## Fighting for Life

It came in the fall of 1887. Mary Towns was up at the break of dawn and looked out at the white sky. Snow had begun falling in lazy lacy patterns, whispering at the window. Mary loved the first snow. She was keeping one eye on the coffee and one eye on the snow. The coffee began to perk, and that delicious aroma permeated through the room. She thought she heard a noise, then reasoned that it was just the perking sounds emanating from the coffeepot. As she reached for the iron fry pan on the wall, she heard the sound again. This time, she knew it was coming from her six-year-old son's bedroom. She hurried to his room.

"Momma," he cried hoarsely.

"What is it, son?" Mary cooed as she rushed to his bedside and put her hand on his head. He was on fire! Immediately, she woke her husband, Calvin. Calvin dressed and rushed out for Captain Parker's cabin. Captain Parker was the only semblance of a doctor in town. He had two years of medical school and had practiced briefly years ago. The story went that he had made a decision causing the loss of a patient. Shortly thereafter he slid into the Adirondacks, melting into the gilded hush of the forested mountains. However, because there was no doctor, Calvin reluctantly aided in times of need. It was bitter cold that morning, and by the time Calvin began the trek to Mr. Parker's dwelling, the snow was slamming in so fiercely that it felt like pebbles hitting Calvin's face.

Calvin finally reached the house and banged on the door. No one answered. He banged again shouting frantically, "Captain, Captain, wake up. My boy is real sick." Finally, after what seemed like hours, he heard rustling inside. The warped wood door squeaked open as the blistering wind sucked Captain Parker's beard out the open door and into Calvin Town's face.

"What, what's the matter, Cal?"

"It's Alfred, Doc. He's real sick. Please come."

"But…."

"I know. You ain't a doctor, but you're all we got. Hurry!" Captain put on his jacket and sped out the door with this frantic father.

"I'll go, but you go get Robert Shaw and bring him to your house. Robert Shaw also practiced some medicine. He had invented a salve made of herbs and other ingredients in a beeswax base, which alleviated certain illnesses. The captain was hoping this medicine would work on Alfred Towns.

"Ok, Doc," Calvin replied as he dropped Captain Parker off and ran toward the Shaws.

That night, both Parker and Shaw diagnosed young Alfred with the grip. Mary and Calvin were relieved. "He'll be hopping around in a few days," Captain Parker predicted as he opened the door. Robert administered his magical medicine assuring the family that Alfred would be fine in no time. Mitchell Sabattis heard about his grandson's illness and walked the short distance to their home. When he saw the little boy, he winced in worry. "I think Alfred is very sick."

"I know, father, but don't you have any medicine that can help him?"

"No, Mary, I don't know this illness," but he made a poultice of mud and herbs and laid it on his head. He did this to calm Mary not because he thought it would help.

It did not help. Nothing helped, and on November 18, Alfred Towns died. Three weeks later, his mother died. The people were anxious because a week later nine-year-old Clara Rose Sabattis became sick with the same

148

symptoms, and she too died. Mary was Clara's sister. Mitchell tried to treat her with old recipes he knew from his grandfather, but they failed, so he called on Calvin Parker again. After looking at Clara, Calvin stated, "This is not the flu or grip. It is something else, and since it is targeting close family members, we have to assume it is highly contagious." He knew it was not Consumption or Pneumonia but feared for everyone's safety because winter was upon them. The Calvin and Sabattis families stayed to themselves as instructed by Calvin Parker, and as the tulips began to blossom, it appeared that the disease had vanished with the winter snow.

By now, Captain Parker had researched through his medical book and discovered that this illness was the dreaded Diphtheria. He feared the coming winter, and his fears were valid because in the fall 1888, Diphtheria took six-year-old Stella Bills, daughter of Truman and Asena Bills. Throughout the winter, the plague disappeared; however, on March 11 and 12 of that year, over fifty feet of snow fell during the Great Blizzard of 1888. Trains were at a standstill. Coal was scarce, and people froze to death. Thankfully, Long Lake escaped the devastation and loss experienced by those living in and around New York City.

By April, people had resumed visiting their neighbors, chatting about how grateful they were that the disease had run its course and the blizzard was over. Little did they know that in June of 1889, the feared Diphtheria scourge would come back with a vengeance not seen before. It was relentless in its pursuit of innocent victims, and the people were powerless to stop it.

In June, eight-year-old Hattie Russell, daughter of Lyman and Angie, had her friend, Charlotte Cole, over to play. That evening, Hattie complained of a sore throat. Angie put her to bed early, thinking it was the pollen. Hattie contacted a sore throat along with the sneezes every spring. During the night, Angie heard her coughing, went to her room, and quickly woke her husband.

"Oh my God, Lyman, she has it."

"But it can't be. It's gone. There hasn't been a case since last fall, and it's June for God's sake."

"Lyman, we need a doctor! We need a doctor now! Maybe it isn't what killed the others, but I know she is burning up!"

It was what killed the others, and on June 27, it killed Hattie. Two days later, Diphtheria took her sister, Carrie. That same day Caroline Cole, age 51, succumbed to the disease, followed by her children Charlotte, Emory, and three years later, Melvin. Meanwhile, the shadow of death hung over the Henderson home, where Delia, 14, died on July 2, Edward, 20, the following day, and John, 7, on July 13th. Their grandfather, old Joel Plumley, did not live to see this travesty. He had passed away peacefully in 1863.

There seemed to be no end to the epidemic. In September of 1889, six-year old Julius Parker awoke in the night coughing. Diana and Richard heard the dreaded sound, "Oh, my Lord, no!" Diana cried as she ran to her son's bed.

Richard took one look at Julius and wept. He knew. By now, the other children were out of their beds. "Stay where you are. Do not come in here," Richard ordered. It was to no avail. Julius died on September 28, along with two-year-old Charlie. Willard, 15, succumbed to the illness on October 1, and thirteen-year-old, Flora, died ten days later. Richard, Diana, and their four other children were spared. In 1890, the Houghton children also perished from the disease, and in 1891, one-year-old Truman and three-year-old Carrie Hanmer succumbed as well. Several more families lost loved ones, including Sarah Keller Rice, but by the next year, the malady had disappeared, leaving in its wake a grief-stricken community. Alba Cole was seen

150

wandering along the lake staring vacantly as if in a trance. He sought out Richard Parker, and they hunted and talked, but the tragedy changed him forever. Richard's wife was devastated. Thirteen-year old Durwood and eleven-year-old Robert Parker stayed silent and close as if waiting for the hammer of death to strike them. On top of having huge losses, these families were isolated from the others. In the midst of this sickness, Lysander Hall became ill, and in 1890 the tough pioneer took his last breath.

Spring brought flowers and gatherings once again, and just when it looked as if the community was healing, Scarlet Fever hit. This initiated an emergency town meeting resulting in the decision to offer a doctor $1000 to come, and in November 1894 Dr. Burch became Long Lake's first doctor. One of his first patients was Zenas Parker, whom many people thought became ill because he witnessed his family cut down by these illnesses. Zenas died in 1896 with his remaining family around him.

Soon this new disease was running rampant in Long Lake and it took Richard and Diana Parker's eighteen-year-old daughter, Etta. Dr. Burch ordered quarantine notices placed on known ill houses, and all those inside were not to mingle with the population. Neighbors went into action securing groceries and medicine for the ill families, cutting and piling wood outside the house and helping in other ways. Later, at a town meeting headed by Henry Kellogg, they proposed that in times of serious illness, quarantine would mean moving the ill to a "Pest House." The town purchased two run-down buildings, one on the Carthage Road (the old Dickenson house) and one on Rice Road.

Eventually, they hired Dr. Decker who in 1902 administered the first vaccination to Raymond Sabattis, son of Charles Sabattis and grandson of Mitchell Sabattis.

In the early part of the twentieth century, with doctors finally on the scene, the Board of Health began questioning the causes of some of these diseases. Doctor Burch pointed to the sawmills as the cause. People were drinking the water filtered through layers of sawdust. The sawmill owners were targeted—the Helms, William Wilson, Ai and Robert Shaw and son, the Robinsons, and Orren LaPelle. The news was not well received, some did clean up, but the streams remained filled with sawdust.

**Long Lake Village, looking toward Deerland (about 1895). Top of the hill is Wesleyan Methodist Church and the school. The building on the extreme left is R. Shaw's store. On the hay rig, left to right: Ai Shaw, Robert Shaw, Michael Cashion, Melvin Gillis, & Kelvin Towns.**

On the other hand, the pristine Adirondack air was conquering another fatal disease, Tuberculosis. Doctor Trudeau had come to his beloved Adirondacks to die after being diagnosed with Tuberculosis. Instead, he began to feel better. He discovered that the pure Adirondack environment was the cure for TB. People built sunrooms on their houses, and the stricken healed on these porches. They opened an institute in Ray Brook, New York, that housed many of the ill. This brought even more people from the city, and once again business blossomed in Long Lake. The wealthy began to notice this peaceful paradise in the corner of upstate New York.

# Chapter 22

## The Little Town that Almost Was—Long Lake West

There had been little activity in the area west of Long Lake since pioneer David Smith left Smith Lake for the lure of the West. In the 1890s, William Vanderbilt purchased vast amounts of land in this area, allowing his son in law, Dr. Seward Webb, to build a magnificent lodge on the lake. This move persuaded Dr. Webb to extend the Mohawk and Malone Railroad lines into the area. The railway station also served William C. Whitney, ex-secretary of the Navy, who located to the northern part of the township, while Webb's Nehasane Park Association set up further south. A major setback occurred in spring of 1897--a severe storm practically destroyed the roadway from the railway station into Long Lake. This did not deter Vanderbilt. Instead, he hired men to fix the road, and soon carriages resumed carrying passengers from the train station to Long Lake.

The train depot location was a logical place for a community to take root, and it did. The little community of Long Lake West was born, and by 1907 the Peoples Hotel, run by George Dukelow, was booming. Shortly thereafter, Dana Bissell purchased the hotel and renamed it Wilderness Inn. Lewis Jennings, from Long Lake, ran a store, built sleighs, and ran the stage line. He recalled telling his wife, Margaret, that they were moving to Long Lake West. Her response was, "When do we go?" Shortly thereafter, the town grew to approximately twenty-five buildings, including barns, stores, a post office, and the train depot. Lewis and Margaret rented a lovely frame house from Augustus Low. In fact, all the homes in Long Lake West were frame homes.

Although this was a remote community, it did not entirely escape the disease that hit the Town of Long Lake, and on February 7, 1903, quarantine was placed on Dana Bissell's hotel. The remoteness of the location made quarantine orders difficult to enforce; therefore, on February 23, 1905, the Town Board of Health empowered Dr. F.S. Decker, health officer, to hire guards to keep watch on the quarantine at Long Lake West. When the doctor lifted the quarantine, Dana sold the hotel to Abbot Augustus Low who owned a vast sugar bush industry. Patrick Moynihan, a successful lumberman who cleared and built roads, lived in town and owned buildings that stored lumber, dynamite, kerosene, horses, and equipment.

Margaret loved her new home built on the other side of the tracks from the store and post office. Every day since shortly after three-month old Arthur was born she walked to the post office and chatted with her friends on the way. On the morning of September 25, 1908, the town was awash in September sunlight. A gentle breeze trickled through the new autumn leaves as Margaret made her way down the worn dirt path.

"Morning, Mr. Low."

"Morning, Margaret, and how is Arthur this morning?" He looked down at the newborn.

"Oh, he's a good baby. He certainly keeps me busy."

"Well enjoy him while you can. It won't be long, and he'll be going down to the schoolhouse." They both looked toward the red schoolhouse surrounded by green grass and backed by several giant hemlock trees.

"Oh, yes, but not too soon. Well, I best get back and start lunch."

"Have a nice day, Margaret."

"You too," Margaret replied as she continued her walk. She scanned the horizon. Reports of fires in the

Saranac Lake area had come through on the telegraph the week before. She thought of those poor people. Some had lost their barns, some even their houses. The sky was clear. The white birches stood elegantly against the sky seeming to touch the little wisps of clouds entering from the east. Shattering this quietude, she heard a faint rumble followed by the piercing whistle of the train.

Arthur began to wiggle in his carriage. By the time she reached the post office, Art was squealing and crying because of the noisy train. Margaret picked him up, cradled him and he soon fell back to sleep. She hurried out of the post office, hustling over to the tracks so she could speak with the engineer. After the engineer stepped down from the train Margaret asked, "What is the word on the fires up north?"

"Not good. This summer was a dry one. They thought Vermontville was a goner, but it escaped. As he exited the cab, he remarked, "Trouble is that when they felled all the trees, they didn't burn the remnants. There's a lot of brush around."

Margaret looked across the street down by the schoolhouse and scanned the landscape along the tracks. There were piles of dead limbs and brush lying around; however, they periodically had cleaning days when they removed the brush close to the tracks. "I guess we're pretty safe here, but maybe we should have another brush clearing day and clear a little more land."

"Not a bad idea. Some of these little fires have been close."

"Oh, my, are we in danger?"

"No, not now. They're all out." Margaret walked away wondering if he had told her the truth. During the past five years, Margaret had smelled smoke many times. The sparks off the trains could ignite the brush and start fires along the tracks. She knew there was a fire on Christie's

156

Bear Pond that had been burning for two weeks. That was close enough. She walked over to the barn, found Lewis, and asked him if they should be worried. He assured her that a telegraph had come in on Friday notifying them that all fires in the vicinity were out.

"Okay, good. We'll see you at noon." Two days later, the Adirondack Express passed through town between noon and one o'clock. Men from the New York Central fire train crews, who had been fighting the fires, were preparing to return to Utica in the morning. They were eating lunch at the Wilderness Inn. They never finished their lunch. A southwest wind raised up, ignited some embers, and within one hour, Long Lake West was no more.

When the fires came barreling through the town, the fire train crew ran out and grabbed their hoses, trying desperately to fight the fire.

"Oh, Lord!" screamed Margaret as she ran out the door and saw the hose in two firefighters' fists melt off in their hands. She rushed into the house snatched Art out of his crib and began throwing items into a basket. Suddenly, Lewis burst through the door. Smoke billowed in behind him.

"No! No time, Margaret! We have to get out!" He grabbed her and Art and rushed them out the door. Through a veil of smoke, she saw animals fleeing and people running and pushing. One couple had piled some items on a wagon and had to flee because the flames took over their possessions. "There is a rescue train," Lewis shouted. "You need to board now!" As they ran to the train car that would take them to Horseshoe Lake, Margaret could hear the terrifying roar of fire and cracking trees. This monster was roasting anything in its path. The flames were so high that she could see no end to them. She was so terrified that Art would suffocate that she dropped the only shawl she had, focusing on saving herself and her baby.

After boarding the train, they sat down beside a woman who was screaming hysterically, "My boys, my boys!" Her teenage boys were in the woods. "Please don't leave without them!" she screamed. Finally, the engineer told her that they had to leave. The wheels began to roll just as the boys came running out of the woods. The engineer slowed the car down while they jumped on.

After Lewis had deposited his wife and son on the car, he turned to leave. "What? Where are you going?' Margaret asked in disbelief.

"I've got to try to save the horses."

"No," Margaret screamed, "no, you do not!"

"Margaret, there are over 200 horses in that barn, and I am just going to open the barn door and drive them up the tracks. I will be right behind you." Before Margaret could protest again, he was gone, lost in the heavy smoke. She held Art close to her and cried.

Lewis, Fred Clark, and some of the other men raced to the barn and opened the doors. They moved the horses out and started running them up the tracks. Suddenly, a huge wall of fire flared up straight in front of them, sending the horses scattering in different directions. The men now raced through the woods to a clearing just north of town. The train picked them up and took all of them, to Horseshoe Lake. However, Horseshoe soon became a danger zone so the rescue train took them on to Tupper Lake junction where they were given lodging.

The train took all to safety except one—James Barry. James was in the woods and had reached Long Lake West a minute too late to catch the relief train. He sought refuge in a freight car parked on the north end of the village. James prayed as he crouched low in the corner of that boxcar knowing that at any moment, the flames would reach him. He could hear the trees crashing down in the woods, and the cows and horses howling in agony. The smoke made him cough and cry, and the stench of burning flesh sickened him. When the dynamite in the shed exploded, it felt as if his eardrums had shattered like broken glass. All went silent after that. Fortunately, inside that boxcar, James found a case of whiskey. He grabbed a bottle, twisted open the cap and began to drink, waiting for the inevitable end of his life. It did not come on that day. By a strange freak of fate, this boxcar was the only wooden thing left intact after the fire. Not until the hissing stopped and the heat subsided did James stagger out of that car. He scanned the scene. There was nothing but black; nothing but charred remnants of boxcars, buildings, animals, and wagons. He crawled back into the boxcar, took another slug, and another until he entered sweet oblivion. The first arrivals found him passed out in the boxcar.

Since everything, including the telegraph office, was annihilated, it took time for the rest of the country to learn about the fire. The next day, Lewis came back to see what could be salvaged. There was nothing left to take.

Long Lake West grew from its ashes but remained a small community. They named the new community Sabattis.

**Durant family travelling to Long Lake West**

**Long Lake West, 1908, after fire.**

159

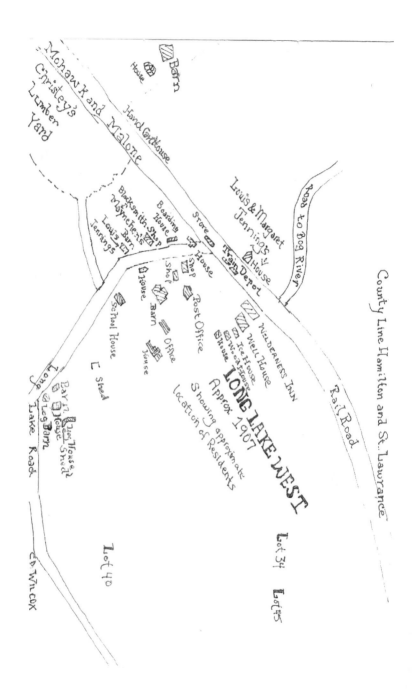

Mohawk and Malone

Christey's Lumber Yard

House

Barn

Hand Car House

Louis & Margaret Jennings V House

Road to Bog River

Boarding House
Blacksmith Shop
Myrick's Barn
Louis Jennings

Store

House

Train Depot

Shop

Shop

House

Post Office

Barn

Office

House

Well House
Ice House
Wood House
House

WILDERNESS INN

School House

L Shed

Long Lake Road

Barn
House
House Shed
L Leg Barn

Ed Wilcox

LONG LAKE WEST

Approx. 1907

Showing approximate
location of Residents

Lot 34    Lot 45

Lot 40

County Line Hamilton and St. Lawrence

Rail Road

160

# Chapter 23

## Into the Twentieth Century

The twentieth century began with a bang. On September 6, 1902, the president of the United States, William McKinley, was shot at the Temple of Music in Buffalo, New York. He was immediately taken to the hospital where he died of wounds to the head and abdomen. He had been shaking Leon Czolgosz's hand when Leon shot him. At that moment, the vice president, Theodore Roosevelt, was climbing Mt. Marcy in the Adirondacks. After the news reached Mr. Roosevelt, he rushed down the mountain and climbed into a horse-drawn carriage. Long Lake folks were chattering for weeks about who in Newcomb drove Theodore Roosevelt to the North Creek train station. There were whispers and stories raging on about how President Roosevelt had stopped at the Lake House as well as at the Sagamore Hotel.

Now Long Lake was blooming like a flower with the Sagamore Hotel and Lake House in full swing. Clarence Fuller and Orren LaPelle managed a series of dances at Pecks Opera House in the Sagamore Hotel. Ernest and Delbert Stanton had taken carpenter jobs at the Lake House. Unfortunately, soon after they secured the jobs, the Lake House burned to the ground. Stephen Lamos, builder, casket maker, and guide, was hired to rebuild the hotel.

Meanwhile, Lewis and Margaret Jennings did rebuild in Long Lake West but within a short time went back to Long Lake. He and his brother Harrison purchased the ten-year-old Lake House, renamed The Adirondack by the previous owner.

The first pioneers took their final rest in the new cemetery, and the new old guides rocked back in their chairs on the porch of barber Adolphus LeBlanc, whose business sprang up across from the Long Lake Hotel. George Smith bought property across from The Grove, now named Deerland by the new owner, Albert Brown.

With the Buttercup long forgotten, George Smith turned out several steamboats from his shop. A large lumber company, Norwood Lumber, partly owned by lumberman Ira Hosley, commissioned George to build a tough steam ship for logging. George built the boat, and young Elizabeth Sullivan christened it, "The Iris." Sam Farr was the engineer. The Iris towed huge log booms down Long Lake. In the spring, they released the big dam at the foot of Forked Lake in preparation for sending the logs down.

Another new settler on the scene, Len West, watched as The Iris approached the old suspension bridge across Long Lake at Pine Island. Sam and his men had to drop the smokestack by a hinge to allow the craft to pass under the bridge. At the narrows, under the bridge, the log booms had to be rolled through, which involved towing one side of the log boom ahead, then hooking on further back and drawing the same side forward. The whole boom turned counter-clockwise, gradually passing through the narrows.

As the logging business made its way into Long Lake, so did the church business. Several people became dissatisfied with the Wesleyan Church, but they were not Catholic. They wanted to start a new church; therefore, in October of 1900, Stewart Irving, Walter Jennings, John Robertson, and Robert Hartson became the central figures in organizing The Methodist Episcopal Church. John and Mattie Anderson, from Newcomb, donated the land next to Foresters Hall, and the new church was incorporated in October 1901.

During the winter of 1901-1902, while Patrick McSweeny was road commissioner, the town built a suspension bridge to replace the deteriorating float bridge. They built a smaller single-span bridge a third as long as the main bridge to connect Pine Island with the south shore, directly west of Hotel Adirondack. Beecher Wilson built a magnificent stone entrance into a forest preserve purchased by the wealthy Walker family, and Warren Cole began building guide boats in his shop on Deerland Road north of The Grove.

In 1905, the population of Long Lake was now supporting four blacksmiths, among them Lyman Beers, Walter Jennings, and Howard Hanmer. Up the hill from the blacksmiths were Joe and Margaret Sabattis' Variety store and Taxidermy Shop and Mrs. James Braley's millinery store across the street. Clarence Fuller opened a store on the lake at the bottom of the hill and built a large pillared house halfway up the hill across from the beautiful domed Methodist rectory. Down the road toward the Long Lake Hotel, across from the ball field, John McAveigh ran a pharmacy in the old Joe Rowe place. Soon, William Hanmer opened another general store there and turned the top floor into a dance hall. Frank Plumley, son of Honest John Plumley, built a bed and breakfast in the home previously owned by Amos Hough. It was diagonally across the road from The Gables. He called it "The Inn on the Hill."

John and Catherine Rice bought the Kellogg property and opened the home up to boarders. The Kellers remained on the same land though they moved the house further up on the hill.

Lavonia and Benjamin Emerson ran the Long View cabins and hotel, turning them over to their sons, Wallace and James, in early 1900.

Foresters Hall, across from the post office was booming on dance night, and Judge Timothy Sullivan's Store along the lake housed a modern telegraph and telephone office. One day Harry and Jessie Helms Stone strolled into the Judge's store inquiring about the new-fangled talking machine.

"Judge, what is that contraption I've been hearing about?" Harry inquired. "You know, that machine where you can talk to other people." Harry was a large man who drew attention to himself wherever he went. Judge Timothy had watched him perform in several minstrel shows.

"And good morning to you too, Harry. Jessie, how are the school children behaving?"

She laughed, "Oh, they are fine, Judge, but Harry's got it in his head that we have to have this machine."

"Well, several people in town do have them. They sure help if there is an emergency. Come with me." They followed him over to the counter. "This is your contraption, Harry. It is called a telephone." He picked it up and handed it to Harry. "You rent it, and we install it." Harry looked it over and then gave it to Jessie.

Always the practical and skeptical, she asked, "Does it really work?"

"It sure does." With that, the judge showed them how to use it and scheduled the install for the next day.

"And you say it works for sure?" Jessie asked again.

"For sure," related the judge. They bought it, and the judge's son, John, came to install it the next day. As soon as John left after installing the telephone, Jessie picked it up and tried to call the operator. She tried several times to no avail. Harry came to her aid, and he too failed to get anyone on the machine.

"I don't know, Jessie, I'll talk to Tim tomorrow."

"Well, I'll talk to Timothy today!" Jessie retorted as she yanked it off the wall, marched down to Sullivan's store with it, and told the judge to keep it until he could provide better service. It would be quite some time before Harry and Jessie had one of those contraptions in their house.

Despite the problems with communications, people continued to settle in Long Lake, keeping local builders and masons such as Walter Reid, Steve Lamos, William Duane, Beecher Wilson, and Howard Hanmer busy. One hot summer day, a young man wandered into town looking for work. He stopped at Howard Hanmer's blacksmith shop and met Carrie Hanmer just closing the door. There was a little red-haired girl tugging at her arm, apparently wanting to stay in the shop. Carrie latched the door, stood up, and almost ran into the silent youth.

"Oh my, excuse me. Uh, my husband is not here." Carrie looked him over. He was tall, dirty, skinny, and did not look a day older than fifteen. "Haven't seen you around here before, young man," Carrie spoke up as she pulled the child closer to her.

"Uh, no ma'am," the young man finally uttered, taking off his hat and holding it nervously between his hands. "I've come looking for work."

"For work? Where do you come from at such a young age?"

"From Westchester County, Ma'am. I heard about this place from the counselor at my orphanage. He told stories about coming up here in the summer so I always knew when I got out, I would come here." The young man looked up at Sabattis Mountain, turned, and pointed to Owlshead Mountain. "I never knew about mountains; I mean, what they looked like. Counselor Alan was sure right. They are a sight to behold."

Carrie immediately began warming up to this young fellow. He was quite articulate. "I am Carrie Hanmer, and this is my daughter, Hulda. We welcome you to Long Lake.

Now, what is your name?" Just then, Howard came back from LeBlanc's barbershop.

"Hi, Carrie." He picked up Hulda and turned to face the boy. "Hello there, I'm Howard Hanmer, and who might you be?"

The boy held out his hand and shook Howard's hand. "My name is Fred, Fred Burns, and I need a job. Thought you might be able to use another hand."

"Yes, Howard," Carrie interjected, "he came because the counselor at the orphanage he is from talked so well about our town."

"Well, Fred, I don't need any help myself but…."

"Howard, how about Lena Bissell? I was talking to her yesterday, and she said she was looking for someone to help around her property. I don't know what she needs done, but it is work."

"No matter, Mrs. Hanmer. I don't care. I'll do anything. Where is it?" Howard gave him directions to the Bissell property. James and Lena hired him as a chore boy.

One October day, as he was digging a ditch through hardpan soil, he stood up, looked around, and thought to himself, I feel as if I am living inside a painting. I can't believe that all of this is real. His eyes dropped from the horizon, and he stared at the rocks on the edge of the black soil he had unearthed. He pulled the shovel back and once again bore down hard, sinking the shovel through the matted roots into the rock hard soil.

As the modern world marched in, the pioneers marched out. The great Indian guide, Mitchell Sabattis had a stroke and died on April 17, 1906, a year before the birth of his granddaughter, Grace, who married Canadian newcomer, Harold Brown. The church was filled with mourners for this wise warrior who left his footprints throughout the forests of a once silent land. One year later, Robert Shaw died after building a large boarding house on

Shaw's Pond, and by 1899, David and Christine Keller rested peacefully beneath Keller hill under the shadow of Kempshall Mountain.

Long Lake, at the turn of the century, had weathered the storms of starvation, death, and disease. These rugged strong-minded people were willing to do the seemingly impossible to survive. Though some families faded into ashes and some moved out west, on a clear spring day, when you wandered up to the Keller farm, you could witness young Lawrence at the reins of the plough horse, turning the soil that began a settlement on the edge of nowhere. As the first settlers faded into the Adirondack soil, their sons and daughters married and continued surviving in the little backwoods community, ever mindful of the sacrifices made by their ancestors.

**Lake Drive. Cobblestone on right. Hanmers' store, top.**

**From Newcomb Road. Andrew Sullivan's blacksmith shop on left. Wesleyan Church on hill.**

**Main Street**

**Helms & Smith Hotel wooden sidewalk**

169

**1900, Looking west from the Kellogg House
Pine Island on left.**

**William Hanmer's Grocery Store**

Barber shop, Cunningham's Store & café

1910, Cobblestone, lower left. Wesleyan Church on Carthage Rd. (Deerland Rd.)

**Hulda Hanmer Hart**

**Ike Robinson**

**Mitchell Sabattis**

**Warren Cole & Lennox West**

**Smith & Helms Hotel porch steps, around 1912**

**Jessie Stone, 1891**

**David Keller Home, 1895**

SCHOOLHOUSE, DISTRICT # 1 (ABOUT 1890), LONG LAKE, N. Y.
IT WAS LOCATED ON THE PRESENT HALE HOUGHTON SITE AND
ABANDONED ABOUT 1900.
FROM LEFT TO RIGHT, FRONT ROW: 1-AMY DUTT?, 2-AGNES LAPELLE,
3-ALFRED LAPELLE, 4 WALES LAPELLE, 5 ANDREW GATES, 6 -UNKNOWN,
7-AMY PALMER?, 8-TEACHER-MISS MILLER?, 9-FANNY LAPELLE,
10-UNKNOWN, 11-UNKNOWN. ORIGINAL SUPPLIED BY MRS. H. HOUGHTON
H.I.B, 1964

**Post Office and store—around 1912**

173

**Catherine & John Rice**

**Left, Smith & Helms Hotel (Hoss's), right front, Robert Shaw house (Jennings), right back, Dolph LeBlanc's barber shop, cobbler shop, store, café, About 1900.**

**Cyrus Palmer &
John Lapell Sr.**

**Charles Bailey
Hanmer, Constable**

**Richard T. Parker (son of Zenas), and
wife**

Keller Family-1870-Front Left-Right-Rowley, John, M-
Charles, Sarah, David. Back-Roselen, Amelia, Almyra

Benjamin and Lavonia
Stanton Emerson

Benjamin Emerson

Long span bridge with scow underneath

Roy Hosley Home—Deerland lumberman

**Robinson House & Mill**

**The Buttercup**

## Acknowledgements

I wish to acknowledge several people who helped me with s book. I appreciate the Frances Seaman family for donating her pers to the Long Lake Archives, which also contained Jessie one's historical writings. I spent many hours searching through e extensive papers left by these two women. I would like to ank Hilary LeBlanc II for his newspaper research and his onderful supply of photos. I appreciate Raymond Smith's tensive genealogical research, which aided me in comparing search data. These two men were prompt, supporting, and lling to help, and I am grateful for their contributions to the ok. I thank Roberta (Bobbie) Parker Nadeau for her time and igence proofreading the manuscript. Jean Cooney Lyman, thank u for your cemetery research and for trusting me with your onderful book of stories and family history. Will Burnett, I am preciative of your time in escorting me to some of the places itten about in the book. Also, thank you to my friend and his n on South Pond for giving me the grand canoe tour exploring e pond that attracted the first settlers. I wish to acknowledge ist, Robin Weiss, for her incredible map illustrations. Thank u, God, for allowing me to live and write in these magnificent lirondack mountains. Thank you to Editor, Martha Francis, for reeing to edit the book and getting it back in record time. ecial thanks to my sister, Venita, for patiently working with me rough the revisions.

# References

Aber, T. & King, S. (1961). *Tales from an Adirondack County*. Prospect, New York: Prospect Books.

Aber, T. and King, S.(1965). *The History of Hamilton County*. Lake Pleasant, New York: Wilderness Books.

Becker, H. (1955). *Long Lake, Shaw*. Blue Mountain Lake, New York: Blue Mountain Lake Museum.

Becker, H. (1965). *A History of South Pond* Origin of Long Lake Township. P 95.

Bissell, T. (2012). Endion. *Long Lake Historical Society Newsletter*. (February) Retrieved from www.llarchives@frontiernet.net

Burnett, Charles. (1932). *Conquering the Wilderness*. Norwood, Massachusetts: Pimpton Press.

Calvary United Methodist Church (1899-1946). Record Book #1.

"Did Not Know Danger was Nearby." (1908, Oct. 15). *Fulton County Republic.*

Donaldson, A. (1921). *History of the Adirondacks* (Book I and II). New York: The Century Co.

Emerson, L. (1840-1928). Early Life at Long Lake. Long Lake, New York. Lavonia Stanton Emerson.

Engles, V (1930). *Adirondack Fishing in the 1930's*-Native Squaretails.

Graham, F. (1871). Adirondack Park, A Political History. *Forest and Stream.*

Granger, P. (2003). *Adirondack Gold*. Thurman, New York: Beaver Meadow Publishing.

Hamilton County New York Gen Web. (2000-2013). Long Lake. Retrieved from www.hamilton.nygenweb.net.

Headley, J. (1849). *The Adirondack or Life in the Woods*. Scribner, Armstrong and Co.

History of Long Lake Wesleyan Church (1855-2008). Viewed March 16, 2012. Retrieved from *http://longlakewesleyan.wordpress.com*

Jennings, V. (1991, Oct. 23). 1908 Forest Fire, which wiped out Long Lake West remembered as "Most Destructive." *Tupper Lake Free Press* pp. 1, 14.

Loane, E. (1962). *Diary of an American Boy*. Mineola, New York: Dover Publications.

Long Lake Class of 1990. Special Edition, <u>An American Classic</u>. Long Lake, New York. Long Lake Central School.

Murphy, J. (2000). *Blizzard! The Storm that Changed America*. New York: Scholastic Press.

Murray, W. (1970). *Adventures in the Wilderness*. Blue Mt, NY. Adirondack Museum.

"Rain Helps Check Adirondack Fires. (1908, Sept. 29). *New York Times.*

Seaman, F. & Stone, J. (1976). <u>Long Lake, A Brief History.</u> Long Lake, New York: Town of Long Lake.

Seaman F. (1980-2005). Long Lake, personal written communications. Long Lake, NY: Long Lake Archives.

Seaman, F. (1992, Aug 4). Adirondack guides hold a special place in history. *Hamilton County News*. P 3.

Seaman, F. (1997, Sept. 2). A Look at Illnesses, Doctors, and Pest Houses. *Hamilton County News*. P 17.

Seaman, F. (1997, Sept. 2). Long Lake at the turn of the century. *Hamilton County News.*

Seaman, F. (2002). *Nehasane*. Utica, New York: Nicholas K. Burns Publishing.

Seaman, F. (2003) *Adirondack Explorer. Vol* 5( #4).

Shaw G. & Shaw R. (1842-1900). *Tahawus-Newcomb and Long Lake*. Blue Mountain Lake, New York: Blue Mountain Lake Museum.

Stone, J. (1954-1979). Long Lake., personal written communications. Long Lake, New York: Long Lake Archives.

Swinney, H. (1970). Rifles. *Adirondack Life*. (Spring). Pgs. 44-48.

The Great Blizzard of 1888. *Wikipedia*. Accessed March, 2013. www.wikipedia.org

Timm, R. (1989). *Raquette Lake, A Time to Remember*, Utica, New York: North Country Books.

Todd, J. (1845) *Long Lake*. Pittsfield, MA: E.P. Little Press.

Verner, W. (1984). A History of the Adirondack Forest Preserved. *Adirondack Life*. (May/June). PP. 38-44.

"Village Wiped Out" (1908, Sept. 28). *New York Sun*.

Williams, E. (1833). Drastus, P. William's Diary. Collections of Vermont Historical Society. Barre, Vermont: Vermont Historical Society. 05641-4209.

Yaple, C. (2011). *Foxey Brown*. Cortland, New York: Charles Yaple.